Witch Shield

Guardians of Chaos

C.D. Gorri

Dedication

To the seekers, the defiant ones, the ones who know they are special and rock out to their own beat.

We knew the second we saw you; you were unique, and we love you for it...

xoxo, C.D. Gorri

Copyright

Witch Shield
Guardians of Chaos Book 5
by C.D. Gorri
Edited by BookNookNuts
Copyright 2022 C.D. Gorri

STOP! Before you go, sign up for my newsletter and get the latest on my releases, giveaways, freebies and more.
SUBSCRIBE HERE

Blurb

She's on a mission to prove magic exists. He has to change her mind.

What happens when a Witch falls for a feisty normal bent on outing the single most vital secret in the known universe?

Egros must convince Elena's mate's sister to stop her investigation into the supernatural world. The cunning female is too smart to bespell. He'll just have to try the old fashioned way.

Margo Wells has done the unthinkable. The human woman has tracked her brother all the way to the

Guardians of Chaos' Keep, and she's not leaving without proof magic exists. All her life, Margo was different. With this revelation, she's finally found vindication.

Will Egros put a stop to the infuriatingly beautiful woman's investigation, or will he lose his heart instead?

Guardians of Chaos Pledge

I am the watcher in the storm.
I am the sword who strikes true.
I am the iron shield.
I protect against those who seek to control the wild
nature of magic.
I am the guardian of chaos.
To thrive, we must be free.
From chaos comes creation.

Prologue

Many years ago...

Egros closed his eyes, not even bothering to block the blows from the other children in the yard. He hadn't done anything to deserve it, but he took it all the same.

This wasn't the regular school recess bullying that he'd seen on after school specials when his father was not home to scold him for watching *normal* television. Witches weren't normals, even if they could pass more easily in society than other supes. Some even went to regular schools and universities.

But not Egros. The Pyke Coven heir did not attend any ordinary school, and the boys who were alternately kicking and punching him while calling him all manner of crude names were not ordinary children.

Oh, they hated him the same way normals hated their peers. With complete and absolute prejudice, and with no one particular reason. He felt their scorn rain down on him with every blow and curse word.

Maybe it was simple jealousy. Maybe they felt threatened by his family name. Or perhaps, it was just sheer stupidity. He contemplated all possibilities while doing his best to protect his nose and teeth from sustaining permanent injury.

The boys ranged in age from Egros' own thirteen years to sixteen and maybe older. Perhaps they could have been friends in some other reality. But not in this. Not where Egros Pyke was smarter, richer, and more powerful than any one of them.

Quiet and studious, he did not ready to anger the way the other boys did. His magic was too great for him to give in to typical hormone induced aggression. Egros knew better. Had been taught better by his now gone mother.

No, he could not lash out, even if he wanted to. Egros Pyke had to maintain control above all else. Even revenge.

The truth was, if you combined the students currently stomping on him, Egros would still outdo them all when it came to money, through no fault of his, brains, which his extensive reading could take credit for, and power, some of which he was born with, the rest he'd inherited, as all Witches do.

All Witches were taught the basics when they were very young. The first lesson number learned was that magic was finite.

There was a limited supply of magic in this plane of reality. It could be reused, recycled, and willed to another. A practice that Witches in particular knew how to do. Passing one's own store of magic to another not of their line was rare, but possible.

The most common way for a Witch to gain his or her magic was to inherit magical stores from an ancestor, usually a parent. Then he or she would continue the tradition of passing it on from one generation to the next.

Magic could theoretically be bartered, sold, or given away to another. But those cases were extremely rare. Some Witches were greedy and grasping, just like normals. They wanted more magic than their lot and sought ways to procure it.

The best way to ensure more power was to marry into a Witch family renowned for their strength. Just like his father had done when he'd married Egros' mother.

An opportunistic Witch, Bartholomew Pyke had taken lead of their Coven from his father before him, but leaders needed power. The Pyke family had nearly depleted their own magical stores years ago.

Bartholomew was not satisfied with what he had, and so, he'd found a young, trusting Witch to be his bride. Egros' mother had been in the area visiting family. Young, naïve, and trusting, she'd been seduced by Bartholomew into a loveless marriage that had been the death of her. Literally.

Igraine Renaldo had been barely twenty, sweet and pliable. She'd used her incredible magic primarily to grow things. Plants, trees, and flowers native to the New Jersey forests were her specialty. Herbs however, were her favorite.

She'd taught Egros the importance of balance when he was barely old enough to walk in the back of their always cold house. No matter how high she'd set the thermostat, Egros always found it bitterly cold inside the Pyke house. Her herb garden was the only place he'd ever felt warm.

Bartholomew Pyke was not known for warmth or feelings of any kind. Especially not towards his awkward son. After his mother's death, things had only gotten worse.

He supposed he should thank his dear old dad for the way he could take the beating he was currently receiving without a single flinch. His present abusers were only kids, after all. Just like Egros, but not. Of course, everyone had their differences.

Most Witches dressed like normals in jeans and t-shirts touting their favorite teams or bands, but not Egros. His dress was too somber, too plain to fit in.

He wore all black from head to toe. Had done so ever since his mother had died. It was his own rebellion against his father. The only way to get back at Bartholomew Pyke through his own constant mourning for the mother who'd loved him. She'd been the only parent who had ever shown him any affection at all.

Also, unlike his peers, Egros did not flout rules. He had nothing to prove by going against authority figures with gags and pranks. His own rebellious plans were too serious, too important for such triviality.

"Why won't you cry?" One of his assailants shouted, kicking him harder.

But Egros was beyond pain at the moment. He'd

managed to close off that part of his brain, losing himself in thought. He could blast them all with a single twitch of his finger, but he wouldn't. Magic was not allowed to be performed outside of class until a Witch had reached the legal age of sixteen years as set forth by the Council of Covens.

No. Underage magic was simply not allowed. There was a simple reason, and that was young Witches were not able to control their spells. Magic was notoriously untrustworthy in someone with no strength to confine it.

So no, Egros did not use magic to stop their kicks and punches, though he could have.

Easily.

The boys didn't see his restraint. Did not understand that he was protecting them by not lashing out. They wouldn't thank him for it either. In fact, he was pretty sure his silence made them hit harder.

Rolling onto his stomach to protect his face, he closed his eyes and waited for the kicks and stomps to end. Egros could take a beating. Had done so for years at the hands of his father.

Imagine what they would say if they knew the head Witch of the Coven Pyke regularly beat his only son and heir. Thoughts of his father filled his head as Tom Riley spit on his back while pummeling his stomach with the hard rubber toe of his sneaker clad foot.

"You gonna just take it, runt?"

"Mommy can't help you, can she? I heard she was a drunk who went and fell out of a window, is that right?"

"Nah, I heard she killed herself because she was ashamed of having this emo fuck for a son!"

"Oooh! Yes! I think he is gonna cry!"

They were wrong, though. Egros never cried. Not even at his mother's funeral. Bartholomew Pyke would not tolerate a son who wept. There was not much the old man did abide. His son, least of all.

The bell rang, signaling the end of the school day, and Egros exhaled. He knew the boys would finally stop tormenting him now that they were free to leave school. One last mouthful of phlegm hit him in the back of the head before they snickered and walked away.

He barely even cared. This petty torment was so much better than what waited for him back home. Egros lay there a moment, reaching out with his preternatural senses to connect with the trees and plants surrounding the courtyard. He always felt better when he connected with nature.

It was soothing somehow, communing with the

trees the way his mother showed him when he was very young. Trees were so often overlooked in today's world. But they were the watchers outliving most people, standing strong and true. Trees were the first record keepers. Sentinels, all of them, standing guard, protecting those under their purview.

Egros often talked to the trees. It was how he knew where to walk, when to stop, when to hide under their shade when his father was rampaging back home. Trees had an excellent system of communication. They could pass knowledge from one to the other through their roots. A little known fact even among the supernatural.

"Egros?" Mr. Bellamy, their teacher, found him curled in a ball on the ground.

Egros sat up slowly, wincing at the pain in his ribs. He looked at the older Witch and waited for the inevitable questions that he knew would come.

"Happened again, didn't it? Why don't you fight back?"

"Nothing happened, sir. May I go to the restroom," he winced as he stood up.

"The bell rang. School's over. Go home Mr. Pyke."

"Thank you, sir."

The bruises would hurt worse tomorrow. He knew this from experience, and yet that was the least of his worries. Egros swatted at the dirt the boys' shoes had left all over him. He hated having dirt on him.

School was over for the day. He walked home through the secret path in the woods only he seemed to know about. Unsurprising, since the other students who attended the private school open only to magical folk, mainly Witches from his Coven, tended to steer clear of the Pyke family heir.

To normals, it was a private school for troubled children with a fiercely steep tuition. That alone kept most people from applying, though there were one or two every now and then. Witches were taught to control their magic at St. Barnabas' School.

But Egros already knew all about control. He had to. Both his parents' lineages were long and powerful. The Pyke Witches had squandered their magic, while the Renaldo family had only grown theirs.

Rumors spread through the coven like wildfire after the unlikely match had been made between his mother, who had been twenty years his father's junior. Though her death, years earlier, had been ruled accidental, Egros always suspected that was not the case.

She had been a victim of his father as well, and shame filled him at his own weakness and inability to protect her. Igraine Renaldo had tried to protect her child, but she'd been no match for Bartholomew Pyke.

His coldness would have been enough to kill her soul, but it was his rage after she'd refused his demands to hand over her magic that had killed her.

After that, Bartholomew had been on the hunt to locate the Renaldo family magic. But Igraine had hidden it well. It was the one secret she'd made Egros keep, and he would until his dying day.

"What is mine is yours, my son. Our secret, okay? He must never have it, promise me?"

"I promise Mother."

"When the time comes, you will know how to unleash your power. Just believe in yourself, my precious boy."

It was the last time he'd spoken to her before going on an overnight retreat with his class. The next day, he'd returned to find her dead and his father angrily demanding him to hand over anything his wife had given to her only child.

"Mom is gone? She's dead?" Egros asked, tears

pouring from his eyes. Fear and disbelief had made him ask questions he knew his father would hate him for.

"*Stop sniveling, boy,*" *his father had sneered, and struck him across the face.*

"*Now, tell me where she hid her magic.*"

"*I don't know, sir.*"

"*Useless brat. Just like her. Get out of my sight!*"

He'd raged for hours until neighbors came to take Egros for the night so Bartholomew could mourn privately.

Mourn. Yeah, right.

Egros knew then what no one else would admit. The head Witch of the Coven Pyke had killed his wife, and no one was going to do a thing about it. Egros was alone. One day, he would pay the man back for what he'd done. He was going to leave the Coven, and when Egros was strong enough, he would return to make his father face justice for his crimes.

It had become Egros' sole motivation for being the best Witch he could be. Over the years, his father had grown more displeased with his son. Even worse, the old man grew enraged and bitter as he remained unable to locate his wife's powers.

So yeah, Egros took his beatings. Suffered them

in silence, just biding his time. He knew where his mother's magic was all along. Even now, his fingers brushed against the uncut amethyst pendant that he always wore around his neck.

The stone was suspended by magic inside a round silver circle and hung from a strand of leather made from dragon skin hundreds of years ago. Not the Shifter kind, but the wild ones who used to roam the earth before knights and crusaders wiped them out.

The pendant was an old family relic on his mother's side. It was also the key to unlocking the Renaldo magic, his rightful inheritance by birth and his mother's wishes. All he had to do was whisper the words his mother had told him over and over again since he'd been a baby.

But Egros knew better than to try that now. If his father knew he held the key to Igraine Renaldo's magic, he would force the boy to hand it over. And that was something Egros would never do. Not willingly.

"Not ever," he whispered fiercely.

Egros' eyes narrowed as he came into the small dried up patch of land behind his father's house. It was his mother's old garden, planted when Egros was just a baby. It was dead now. Just like her.

"*Where is it, eh? Useless boy thinks he can hide it from me. It's mine!*"

Egros heard his father's mad mutterings from outside the open window. The old man was in his room again, tossing his belongings around. Always searching for the thing that would never be his.

Egros turned around and walked back into the woods. He would sit and wait till his father's madness passed, or exhaustion took him into one of his deep slumbers. Either one would be preferable to what would happen should he enter the house just then.

He sat against the gnarled bark of a beech tree and waited, eyes closed, until the still of the night cloaked him in its protective covering. Some magic was just natural, and the woods had always welcomed the Pyke boy.

When he opened his eyes, sensing his father's quiet, Egros saw a black Wolf lying beside him. A Shifter, not a wild beast. One he knew well.

He smiled at Storm and patted his head. Egros was all alone in the world except for this Wolf Shifter. He'd befriended him one day in these same woods not too long ago. Storm had been injured and Egros had healed him.

Now and then he showed up, just to check in.

He always seemed to know when Egros had had a bad day. Like today. The Wolf's name was Hudson Stormwolfe. He was a friend and sort of a protector too, waiting to intervene should his own father prove too rough.

"I'm fine. It was school bullies, nothing else," he told the Wolf.

The beast whined, and Egros looked down and grinned. A brown paper bag was by his leg. Inside, he found a sandwich, apple, and carton of iced tea.

"Thank you, Storm."

Then he ate. Together they stayed in the woods, boy and Wolf, until the sun broke through the trees. Something told Egros not to go home that night.

Good thing too. The next day, he'd returned home to discover his father gone. The Enforcers, that was what they called their own magical police force, were already there. They investigated, questioned Egros, but he remained silent.

A few hours later, Kingston Baldric, leader of Storm's group of Guardians, had come to fetch him. Egros had not said a word while the adults negotiated custody of him. He was still an underaged Witch.

"He has no family, no friends, and no one else

who wants him," the Dragon Shifter stated without inflection.

"Fine. But he has a future here," one of the Coven elders said.

"He will decide his future. Until then, he will stay with us where he will be protected."

That was how Egros Pyke wound up in the Keep of the Guardians of Chaos. The building was old and large, full of hidden power and secrets. Egros could sense magic and mystery.

Power had a unique smell. It gave him a tingling feeling he couldn't quite explain. But he knew he was safe there, and with that revelation, the boy finally exhaled.

"Welcome Egros," Kingston Baldric, Alpha Dragon Shifter, and leader of that group of the Guardians of Chaos said in a kind and even voice.

"Thank you, sir."

"You understand what we do here?'

"Yes."

"And you wish to join us?"

"I do."

"Might I ask why?"

"Because magic needs me. And I will protect it, with my life if necessary."

"Alright," Kingston said, nodding at him. "First,

you will train. Then, when you are a man, and if you still want to, you may make your vow to the Guardians."

"Agreed," Egros said, and shook his hand.

This was his destiny. He felt it in his bones and in the pendant pulsing gently around his neck. Egros was finally right where he belonged.

Chapter One

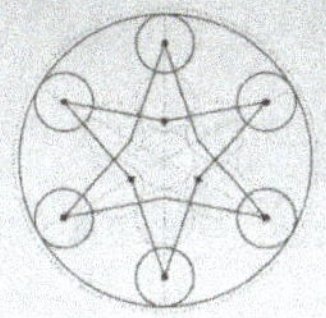

"Margo Wells?"

"Hmm?" Margo's head swiveled right once she'd heard her name.

"Letter for you."

"Oh," she replied. "Thanks."

One of the several uniformed security officers working in the nondescript government building stopped in front of her desk. He checked Margo's badge before nodding, then he dropped the large manilla envelope with the word classified stamped across it in bright red ink on the plain wood surface.

Margo stared at the envelope and shivered once. Her office was always a brisk 64 degrees. She should have worn a sweater, she thought before turning her complete attention to the plain missive the guard had brought her.

She blinked, cleared her throat, and perused the ominous looking package before touching it. It was big, 10 by 13 inches from her estimation. Seemed way too large for the desk she was currently using while working this temporary assignment. It practically dwarfed the small rectangular keyboard on her private laptop.

Margo never used anyone else's hardware. Simply didn't trust it. Besides, she had higher security clearances than most agents could ever dream of. It was easy enough to disguise the super powered laptop to look like the part of the standard Lenovo ThinkPad everyone else used. Was only a matter of stickers, really.

Still, Margo frowned before reaching out to touch the envelope. A sharp pain went through her head, gone before it even registered, and she waited for the brief flash of intuition that usually followed such an occurrence.

For years, she'd had *feelings* when something big was about to happen. Usually, something life-altering. She didn't call them premonitions, though that was as close to the truth as she would allow. Never cared for the word psychic, either. Rang too close to 900 numbers and infomercials for her liking.

Still, these little tidbits of knowledge that sometimes crept into her conscious mind from the great beyond, the ether, or some other such place, were not always good. Some considered them a burden, but she was too cautious to label them that.

Truth was, it had been a long time since she'd shared them with anyone. It just wasn't worth it. How often had she been called crazy by someone she knew after she'd shared a glimpse of their future? Even worse, were the horrified stares and wide berths they'd walk around her if her predictions came to pass, as they always did.

It was a difficult lesson, but Margo had learned to keep her visions to herself very early in life. Oftentimes, she simply ignored them. Like that one recurring dream she'd been having ever since she was a child.

In that dream, Margo was either sleeping or hurt, she could not tell which. But that wasn't why it was so odd. It was the fact she was being carried by a fair-skinned stranger with purple flames engulfing them both that freaked her the fuck out. That strange violet hue matched the ethereal glow that seemed to come from the handsome stranger's eyes.

She could not see his entire face, just that hypnotic, inhuman stare of his. Secretly, she thought it was hot, but that was something she only ever admitted to herself. Didn't matter, anyway. He was a figment of her imagination. A guy that hot simply had to be.

Margo did not know who he was, only his eyes were visible. The rest of his face was hidden by her own poofy crown of curls. She couldn't tell if he was nuzzling her or what.

Whatever.

She did get the feeling he was taking her to safety. That she was, in fact, safer with him than anyone else on the planet. Her own knight in shining, *er*, leather. He wore a black leather jacket. In fact, his entire outfit was black.

Margo had kept that particular vision to herself for almost thirty years. It was just too private to share, and she couldn't be sure if it was only her imagination. Some childish dream of prince charming coming to rescue her or something like it. Besides, Margo didn't need rescuing. She was a kickass woman who was more than capable of saving herself, *fuck you very much* to all the naysayers.

That morning though, she'd seen something else. Over her usual steaming mug of coffee, prepared with one cream, no sugar. Margo had caught a glimpse of this same envelope. Large and plain, sitting on her desk.

Her visions were like that sometimes. Like snapshots someone had just airdropped straight into her brain. Still images. No context.

Frustrating? More often than not. But the years had taught her patience. So, she'd accepted the image, committed it to memory, waited a bit, and *bam*, there it was.

Like magic.

The very same thick manilla sleeve, printed label with her name in bold, no return address, from her vision. There was only one clue as to where it came from. The small stamp at the top left corner portraying a hand holding the world told her all she needed to know.

The envelope had come from Mother.

Not Mother, as in the woman who gave birth to her, but *Mother*, as in her boss. The code name was for the five foot ten inch, three-hundred pound, half-Chinese, half-African American male who ran her department.

Mother made even the stoutest of agents cry with only the slightest hint of his disapproval in the curl of his upper lip. How he got the moniker, she had no idea, and she wasn't interested in asking. The last guy who did got his head put through a wall. So yeah, she was good with not knowing.

He was even scarier than some of the creatures she tracked for him. Assessing the situation, Margo could only come to one conclusion. This was classified. She looked around to gauge her level of privacy before even attempting to open the missive.

Nope. The place was hopping with agents. She rolled her eyes, impatient as always. She could practically hear Logan in her head.

Just chill out, Gogo.

That's what he would say in this instance. Her brother had dubbed her *Gogo* years ago because she was always in a rush and unable to get the words 'Logan go' out of her mouth fast enough. So, it was always '*go go*' until she became *Gogo* herself.

Sigh.

It could be worse. She had a coworker dubbed Head because of the size of his noggin.

Not her fault, she was always looking for what came next. Especially when she could often see the outcome as clearly as if it had happened already. Like the time she'd shoved Logan across the street, saving him from a car that had made a wild turn at the corner where they'd been eating popsicles on a hot July day.

There was no logical reason the then eleven-year-old Margo would have known the car was coming at that precise moment. But she had, and thankfully, that vision had saved her brother's life.

Margo was always getting *feelings* like that. She still listened to the warnings her sixth sense sent her. Even if she'd stopped sharing them long ago.

Who needed another psych eval in their file, anyway? Not this chick.

To the other employees that afternoon at the busy downtown Newark NSA building, Margo was just another law consultant. Just another temporary to fill in on whatever case needed her.

It wasn't unusual to get deliveries at work. Cases overlapped, new materials came in, evidence, dossiers, *etc.* Mail was delivered and sent out all the time. So no, not unusual. Especially when so few lawyers worked in this particular office.

Margo liked her job for that reason. The hiding in plain sight aspect was appealing and thrilling on several levels. But that was her, a complicated mess of conflicting likes and dislikes.

She liked rules, though she flouted them. Adored

court but avoided it. Liked to read but had no time to indulge, and she absolutely abhorred audiobooks. Loved musicals but hated listening to show tunes in the car or anywhere other than while watching a movie or show.

Then there was her greatest love, the unknown, or as she preferred to think of it, the *unrevealed*. Margo had a seriously complex love hate relationship with mysteries. In fiction, they were fine, but in real life, not so much. She'd made it her life's work to uncover the truth about the biggest mystery of all.

Magic.

Yep. Margo Wells, hard ass lawyer and government agent, was hunting for proof that magic actually existed in the world.

Her peers thought her crazy. Hard to believe, since they were all part of the same unit assigned to watch supernatural creatures. Yes, they were real. No, she did not have ready or deliverable proof. It was classified, of course.

Ever since she'd taken up her job with the DPCA, also known as the *Department of Paranormal Creatures and Activity*, she'd come to learn that some of the most widely accepted mysteries and legends of all time were real.

The world might only believe in what they could see, but for Margo, who could see beyond the norm, she believed in something more. What was known as the truth and the actual truth were distant cousins in her world. To think, there was still so much they had to discover, and even more, they had to keep hidden.

If the general public knew how many secret branches of the government actually existed, they'd shit a collective brick. Margo was sure of it. Hell, even the most intuitive conspiracy theorists couldn't fathom the level of deception at work on the daily. But that was life, she supposed. Hadn't she accepted that long ago?

It didn't really matter to her. Lies for the common good were all that held society together sometimes. Margo tended to just accept it for what it was before she moved on.

Her one truth was this: secret government agencies did, in fact, exist, and Margo Wells worked for one of them. That was her reality.

Mother, her boss at the DPCA, had assigned Margo to this NSA office to investigate some of their new cases, searching for any hint of the paranormal. Many of them skated dangerously close to revealing the secrets her agency worked so hard to keep.

She meticulously searched, found, and quietly sent those cases to her agency. The DPCA would step in to handle them covertly. Other cases she found and recognized were sent to secret agents she knew from the other various government agencies of the same ilk.

Yes, they too existed.

Some of them dealt with natural disasters. Others with critical planetary emergencies. And others still handled communications and skirmishes between Earth and beings from other realms, planets, and even solar systems.

Then there was her organization. The Department of Paranormal Creatures and Activity, or the *DPCA,* as they were called. So yes, she sat there disguised as a simple NSA legal consultant in order to do her job. Even as she crept around her desk, strode down the hall, and closed herself inside the closet ripe with janitorial supplies in order to open the strangely ominous envelope, she had to admit she loved it all. The mystery, the action, and the magic.

Especially the magic.

Chapter Two

Okay, so Margo had a vested interest in the findings of her agency. A former US Marine, esteemed lawyer, and all around badass, Margo was not only in the top 1% of her graduating class at Harvard Law. She also excelled in combat and had earned medals for her sharpshooting skills.

Her extreme intelligence and affinity for language had seen her graduate from college three years early and pass the bar exam with only one year of law school under her belt. So, despite appearances, Margo was a Wells through and through.

Neither the color of her skin, nor the fact that her mother was not married to her biological father at the time of conception, birth, or at all, for that matter, could change that. Her parents had simply fallen in lust and bed, in that order, and she was the byproduct.

Her father's family had all but refused to acknowledge her existence at first, even going so far as to try and have her mother moved to a different hospital since she and Logan did, in fact, share the same birthday.

Cassidy Green wasn't much of a mother. She'd worked in law enforcement until her untimely death, leaving little room for her child. No, it was Margo's Aunt who'd taken her home from the hospital. And she was the one who had raised her when Cassidy was killed five years later on assignment.

Both she and Logan's mother, a truly lovely human being, were responsible for her and her brother's meeting. Those two women had been tougher than nails and made damn sure the siblings had ample visitation with one another.

Was that weird?

Maybe. On paper, for sure. But Margo had never felt anything but acceptance and love from either of them or from her twin brother. Hell, if it wasn't for Logan, she could not fathom where she would be right now. Okay, technically, he was not her twin, but the second he'd found out about his sister, he'd demanded time with her. Even after his mother had died, and he'd been barely old enough to form sentences, Logan made sure Grandfather Wells included her in all their family plans and events.

Logan Wells might be her half-brother on paper, as it was true, they shared the same father and had different mothers, but he was her whole brother in her heart.

He was a genius scientist, physician, and a kickass bass player. They'd been born the same day, just minutes apart, and in the same hospital. His poor sweet mother had put up with the knowledge of not only Margo's birth, but she'd made her feel welcomed and loved too. Even agreed to call her his twin, to her secret delight.

But regardless of her mother and his father's infidelity, Auntie Beth, Lily Wells, and Logan were the best parts of her childhood. Margo's own mother was never one to stick around and she'd left her only child in the care of her sweet Auntie Beth more often than not even when she'd been alive.

Lily Wells was her polar opposite and how her husband could cheat on the beautiful and sweet woman, Margo had no idea. But the woman accepted his illegitimate spawn, and for Margo, that meant endless weekends in their enormous house.

Like it or not, the Wells family was *her* family. After the frail woman had passed away, her weekend visits grew far and between, until Logan started pitching fits about it. Despite Grandfather Wells hating her guts, Margo's visits resumed and her relationship with her brother had blossomed.

She loved Logan more than anything else in the world. He understood her, accepted all her quirks, even her weird insights, without question.

Both Wells heirs were gifted. There was no mistaking that. Their shared genetics were responsible, she supposed, but what did that matter?

He chose science as his career, and she chose the government. Breaking into the Supreme Court's mainframe to get access to their court documents was not something she'd encourage others to try, but it had gotten her noticed by certain important people.

Sure, she was better when it came to litigation, but Margo was also something of a skilled hacker. She could get through any firewall or security system she encountered. Only one gave her trouble, but even *Draco Fortis* was no match for her techy skills.

Soon Margo's unusual talents were put to use, and she'd been recruited by a special black ops department that dealt with an entire world that was unknown to society. Classified was a word she'd become very familiar with these last few years working for the DPCA.

She checked the lock on the janitorial closet where she'd gone to open the envelope one last time before tearing it carefully along the fold. She bit back a gasp. The last thing Margo ever expected to see was a picture of her brother in the company of those, those *animals*!

"Oh no," she murmured, frowning hard.

Margo had first learned of the existence of Shifters only a few months ago. People who could morph into animals and were just as wild and dangerous. As far as she knew, which was what the DPCA told her, was that Shifters included Were-wolves and some subspecies of bear.

It was believed a genetic mutation was the reason for such creatures. Margo suspected otherwise, but never voiced it aloud. She was not a fan of being ridiculed for her beliefs. The one time she spoke out, her boss had quickly shut her down.

"Fairytales don't exist, Wells, only monsters," Mother often said.

But nothing could have prepared her for the feelings running through her as she looked at the grainy images of her brother in the company of a pink haired woman. The same woman who, in the next image, turned into a sleek black cat.

Holy cow! Shifters could be cats? That one photograph changed everything. Beneath the pictures was a typed letter with instructions. Mother wanted more info on the cat.

Margo's orders were to collect intel from Logan, but he was her family, and despite what she told her bosses, his safety came first. That meant getting him the fuck out of there.

"Where you off to? Margo? Margo!"

Her temporary NSA team leader, Declan Baudelaire, stopped her on her way down the hall. She looked down pointedly at the soon to be dismembered hand gripping her elbow. Margo did not like to be manhandled.

In fact, touching of any kind was only permitted by invitation only. And desire his having made that suggestion a time or two, she'd firmly refused to get involved with anyone from work. Her mama always told her not to shit where she ate. Besides, office romances were never as kinky or gratifying as they sounded.

To think she'd quit practicing law only two years into her practice and had given up her judgeship all for this. No way she was going to stand there and be questioned by her boss. Not when she was worth twice what he was in the field.

She knew it too. Margo never had a problem with knowing, accepting, and very boldly stating her worth. Had done so with her first job with the FBI. Then again, with the NSA. And now, with the covert DCPA.

She'd had quite the career already, considering she was just in her thirties. But there was one thing Margo did not do, and that was explain herself. Not ever.

"I'm taking a leave of absence, Declan. Two weeks."

"But we're in the middle of---"

"Two weeks," she snapped.

She was already in the parking lot beneath the main building and on her way to rescue her brother. What in the hell had the fool gotten himself into now?

She tied back her curls, the damn things had a mind of their own. Huffing out a sharp breath, Margo threw her car into gear. There was only one thing she loved in the world *almost* as much as her brother.

And that was her *still hot from the factory* Camaro SS convertible in cream blue with performance seats and 455 horsepower engine. The damn thing purred when she turned the engine.

Prrrrr.

But Margo did not take time to appreciate the fine as fuck machine. She flipped switches and waited for the GPS to direct her. The console had been completely redone with her own customized hardware, including some state of the art, not available anywhere, tracking software.

Lucky for her, Logan had no idea she'd microchipped his ass when they'd gone out for his birthday a year ago. He never could go toe to toe with her when it came to booze.

Like a fucking puppy, she'd stuck him with the needle, inserting the tiny chip into his ass that she'd hoped she would never have to use. Should have seen this coming, she thought with a shake of her head.

They both led busy lives, and it was true she hadn't seen him in a while. Guilt had started to eat away at her, but she was just as career focused as he. Another Wells family trait.

Monthly check ins via email did not make up for real sister and brother bonding time they used to share. Even with Grandfather Wells disapproving glare in the background. Margo had always loved her visits with her brother.

He'd been so pale and thin as a kid. She loved holding his hand and looking at the contrast between her gold brown skin and his fair complexion. No one would ever guess they were related. Not unless they looked at their eyes.

Margo had the Wells hazel green eyes, flecked with gold. With her darker skin tone, they practically popped out of her head. She used to hate the way her eyes drew stares, and eventually, questions when she was in her youth. She'd grown accustomed to it, made internal adjustments so it wouldn't bug her.

Being brilliant meant having a thicker skin than most, and as far as Margo was concerned, her mixed heritage was her own damn business. No one else's. She was not interested in debating race, religion, or anything of the like.

Those were human problems, and Margo was in search of something more. Something *unrevealed* to the populace. Something that explained why the hairs on the back of her neck stood straight up when something was about to happen. Or the knack she had for guessing the right number to play at the roulette table. Or when to get off the highway before traffic backed up.

Margo was searching for proof that magic existed, but all that would have to wait. First, she had to save her brother.

"Don't worry, twin, I'm on my way," she muttered.

Chapter Three

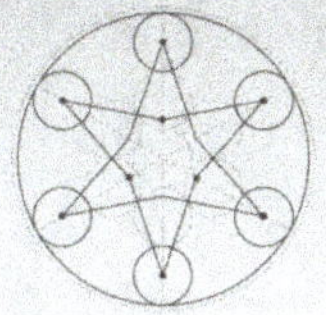

resent...

P Egros sat down in the living room of the Keep. It had been a very eventful day. Elena had claimed her mate and announced it to all, reunited with her father, who turned out to be one of the Assembly, that was like the Council but for Guardians only, and he'd realized he was completely wrong about her choice for a partner. Logan was her fated one, her conpar, and that was something no one could cast asunder.

Afterwards, Holley had gone into labor, and the Guardians welcomed their first offspring in a hundred years or more. Kingston was a father, and they should all be rejoicing. Storm and Furio had opened champagne, nonalcoholic for their mates, now both expectant mothers, and they'd passed out cigars. It was quite the event.

Only, Egros did not feel like celebrating. To be honest, he felt a little bit like an ass.

Okay.

More like a complete and total ass.

He looked at the faces of those around him and his heart squeezed inside his chest. They were almost all paired up. Each of his fellow Guardians had seemed to find their mates, all but Byram, the Vampire, in the last year or so. Yes, he was grateful to the gods for giving him a second chance to remain one of them, but he could not help but feel apart from them all.

Witches did not have fated mates. Not to his vast knowledge, anyway. He'd thought Elena might be amenable to being with him, but even then, it was only a half-assed gesture meant to help the Panther Shifter in her time of need. Of course, everyone thought him in love. He wasn't. Just lonely and perhaps a bit jealous.

How very human of me, he thought with a sneer.

To think he'd almost ruined his life and all because of ignorance and stupidity. And yes, envy too, even if it wasn't the kind everyone thought. It didn't matter. All that mattered was that they'd somehow forgiven him. All of them. Unbelievable. And yet, he was so very grateful.

Elena sat on her mate's lap looking happier than he'd ever seen the female Panther Shifter. Logan Wells, her *conpar,* that was the Guardians word for beloved fated mate, was a brilliant scientist.

He was also a human, or *normal,* as supernaturals tended to call them. Somehow, he fit in with the motley crew of Shifters, a Witch, and a Vampire. They were all members of the Guardians of Chaos, having vowed to keep magic free for all beings.

It wasn't just organizations like the Loyalists who plagued them, but it was the humans too. Truth be told, the past decade had been full of so many technological advancements that keeping magic secret was becoming quite the task. For a male Witch, there was no duty more sacred.

Magic was the single most important secret in the entire universe. A fact that Egros had been taught years ago behind the stone walls of St. Barnabas' School, when he'd still been a member of the Coven Pyke.

He shivered at the thought of his youth and that horrible place. It wasn't the teachers or even the bullies of his school days that made him freeze in place. No, only one man could cause such an intense reaction.

Bartholomew Pyke.

The man had been missing since that fateful day Egros had gone to live with the Guardians. He'd even been declared dead in a court of law. Of course, Egros had never believed his father had run off and wound up dead. Not Bartholomew Pyke. The old bastard was simply too mean to die. Regardless, he'd left the Coven, and lived the life he was meant to be here in the Keep with his fellow Guardians and friends. For the first time in his life, Egros had friends. He hoped he still had them, at any rate.

Recent actions left him riddled with guilt and for a moment, he wondered if he would be banished from the only real home he'd ever known. Guess even a gifted Witch had to wrestle with the green-eyed monster once in a while.

It was not simply jealousy, though that was what they had all assumed. Egros cared for Elena, but he was not in love with her. Not really. She was beautiful, yes. And yes, it was true he'd offered to see her through her heat. But in retrospect, it was because she was his friend.

He simply couldn't bear to think of her in pain. The fact she'd chosen a normal over him had caused him to lash out because of the danger she was putting them all in.

She didn't seem to understand that humans were the single most destructive force in the universe. They were the complete opposite of everything Egros believed in.

Guardians protected magic. The cornerstone of their beliefs was the idea that *from chaos comes creation*, but humans did not abide chaos. They were rigid with structure and schedules. Intolerant of anyone who was different, but they had no qualms about paving nature, leveling jungles needed for something as vital as clean air to breathe, polluting oceans until they were unlivable, chopping down forests, fracking for oil, and those were just their environmental monstrosities.

In his experience, humans were also responsible for curbing creativity, punishing those who dared to be different with derision and hate.

Order. Order! ORDER!

Always calling for order, but the daft bastards did not seem to realize that order was confining. It was restrictive and led to intolerance.

The only thing that came from intolerance was destruction, and that was the root of all evil. Not money or sex or even religion. Not politics either.

Nope. It was humanity's ever increasing appetite for destruction that was pure malice at its worst.

Egros' magic pulsed and buzzed along his skin, and he closed his eyes. He should be feeling joyous. At the very least, contentment. But no. He was anxious.

Their leader, Kingston and his mate, Holley, one of the most powerful Witches he'd ever met, had welcomed their young into the world this very evening. The birth of a half-Witch Dragonling was rare and momentous. It was neither the time nor place to get into one of his moods.

He closed his eyes and counted to three. That tactic still worked after all these years, believe it or not. When he finally reopened them, the purple sparks that had begun to dance along his fingertips were gone.

Good.

The idea his powers were becoming unbalanced was something every Witch, male or female, feared. He still wore the pendant with his magical inheritance locked away. There was no way he could trust himself with the added powers of his mother's family when he could not control what he already had.

Best to keep it locked away, he thought with a frown.

The pendant warmed against his chest and Egros exhaled unsteadily. He could feel the magic there calling to him, and he answered with the only words he could.

Not yet.

It was the additional *maybe not ever* that he kept to himself. Elena's giggle had his head turning in the direction of the *so in love* couple. The Panther Shifter was currently basking in the glow of her *conpar's* affection, and Egros was happy for her.

Truly, he was. She lifted her hand, admiring the pink sapphire ring her mate had given to her, which Egros had magicked to grow and recede as needed when she shifted from Cat to woman.

It was a rare and precious stone, but that was irrelevant. Logan was fabulously wealthy. Not that it mattered. Elena had to be one of the most down to earth women Egros had ever met.

He nodded at her whispered thanks, a bit embarrassed that Logan had given him credit for the spell at all.

Bloody hell.

The gods knew he didn't deserve it. But he replied with a nod, gracious as ever. Egros was just glad his fellow Guardian and her mate were speaking to him at all. Amazingly enough, he had been forgiven by the people he'd hurt the most.

The evening air was chilly in springtime, even as they readied to meet summer. He could hear crickets waking, waiting to rub their wings together, sounding their own mating call. The trees stretched and groaned, their buds tightening with the drop in temperature.

Egros listened to it all, blocking out the noise of those gathered round in the warmth of the Keep. It was the time for birth and renewal, for growth. The whole world seemed waiting to blossom, and Egros knew his job was simply to watch it happen.

Like with his Guardians finding their mates. Like Elena and Logan, a couple who were truly meant to be together. He saw that now, clear as day, and he wished them well.

Shame filled him, and he frowned. He still couldn't believe what he'd almost done. Coming between a supernatural and his or her mate was the worst kind of trespass. For Guardians, a *conpar* was more than a mate.

A conpar was the Guardian's most sacred fated mate. One who was beloved and cherished above all. Anything and everything else were second to that one being perfectly suited for that one lucky Guardian.

Only those most blessed and deserving found their conpar. When that occurred, new stores of magic and powers beyond imagination opened up for the Guardian. The better to protect his or her mate, of course.

Usually, it meant extra strength and endurance, but there were other boons as well. For Storm, it meant blue swirls of magic that allowed him to blink from one location to the next with a mere thought. For Kingston, control over fire and flame was now part of his magical repertoire. Furio's Stallion had powers much like the mythological Pegasus ever since he'd mated his beloved Jessenia.

The *Italian Stallion*, as his fellow Guardians called him in jest, could actually fly with the help of magical wings made of green fire. And Elena had actually become the *Panther Incensed* of legend with pink flames dancing on her skin and coming from her ears.

All these added powers served to make the Shifters in question stronger, faster, and better at their job, which was ultimately to protect magic. In doing so, they were protecting the universe for their *conpars*, making it a better, safer, and more magical place.

A place of pure creation.

Loneliness started to weave its way into his mind. As usual whenever he got into one of his more pensive moods. That hated longing he could not help but feel for someone to call his own tried to overshadow the wonder and happiness he'd felt for his friends.

The pendant around his neck buzzed and hummed, and Egros felt his magic pulsing inside of him. He had to work at keeping his cool, and it was an energy sucking task. More so than a heavyweight champion going twenty-three rounds inside the ring with his equal.

By the time he was finished tightening the screws on the metaphorical box where he put his magic whenever he felt dangerously close to losing control, Egros was sweating.

"You alright?" Elena asked, suddenly.

"Yes," he replied, uttering the lie easily.

He could not tell her the truth. Had to hide the truth from them all. Egros Pyke was just as lonely and unwanted as he'd been as a child. The Witch was unworthy of their company.

No, he would never share their fate. He would

never find his soul mate, his conpar. It simply was not meant to be.

Witches were not the same as Shifters. They did not operate on instinct alone. Shifters were dual natured beings and their animalistic sides used senses Witches simply did not have. He'd often wished he could sniff out his own mate as easily as a Shifter did. Yes, it was sometimes nothing more than a literal sniff. Imagine having the ability to scent things like lies, arousal, and a mate? Amazing creatures, Shifters.

Yes, they used magic, but it was on a different level. Both sides of their natures were always converging and working together. Witches were more like normals in the sense they were not sharing an existence. Magic was inherited or gained, but it was something that needed tending and care. Magic untethered or unlearned was unpredictable and untrustworthy.

Of course, a Witch's relationship with magic was also profoundly different than a Shifter's or Vampire's. Not that Byram shared much info on that. As a male Witch, and the last of his line, Egros had the magic he was born with, or that which transferred to him at birth. He also had access to the stores of magic willed to him by his mother.

His father's magic had not transferred to him at the time of that man's disappearance. Whatever had happened to Bartholomew Pyke, he'd taken his magic with him. And for that, Egros could only thank the hateful man who'd sired him.

He was just fine with what he had, unlike many power-mad Witches. Yes, other creatures wanted power too, but Witches should know better.

"What has you so lost in thought?" Logan asked, disturbing his reverie.

"Oh, nothing," he replied, grateful to the normal.

"Egros is usually a deep thinker. No worries though, love, if you see him struggling just tell him a joke," Elena teased.

It was well known amongst the group that Egros did not get many punchlines. He was far too literal. Looking around at the group of them, he was proud to be part of this group of Guardians who had found not only one, but four of their conpars.

Down the hall, he could hear their Alpha cooing to his new son. Greyson Mount Baldric was the first of the new generation that Egros predicted would be ruling the halls of the Keep sometime very soon.

He did not mind the tiny addition. Even with all the wailing that was bound to keep him up late at night lest the Keep install some extra soundproofing within the walls.

It was all good, though. Children created their own brand of chaos, and to Egros nothing could be more perfect. Kingston was lucky to have found his true fated mate in Holley.

The Dragon had been mated before, or so they had all thought. But the female Dragon had not been his conpar, and the difference was incredible. Holley completed him in a way that could inspire poets. Just imagining it made his mind boggle.

Kingston loved Holley so much he broke curses and battled warlocks for the chance to be with her. And now, the once stoic Dragon smiled and laughed easier than in all the years Egros had known him.

If only I had that chance, Egros thought sadly.

Chapter Four

He needed to get out of there, to break up the monotony of the scenes playing out before him, else he would go mad. How could he act happy all the time when he was utterly alone?

Ugh.

Egros managed to disgust even himself with those selfish thoughts.

"I'm going to go get a drink. Want something?" Egros asked Elena and Logan.

"No, thanks," they replied together.

The couple was all wrapped up in one another, as they should be, and he was tired of feeling like a third wheel. He was getting ready to stand when Furio shouted at him.

"Yo, Egros! You think you can help me set up the artificial lights in the greenhouse for Jessenia?" the Stallion Shifter asked from across the room.

The male Witch was jarred from his many thoughts. A good thing, of course. But before Egros could answer, something flashed outside the window. He narrowed his eyes, raising his hand for Furio to wait a moment when the ready to anger Shifter snorted impatiently.

Then something hit the glass window, causing an explosion that had glass flying everywhere and Egros on his feet. Using magic, he raised an invisible shield that repelled the dangerous shards. Snarling, he was ready to blast the intruder to smithereens until he saw *her*.

"Get the fuck off my brother!" snarled the petite, full human female.

Glossy curls crowned her head, and her golden brown skin glowed in the lamplight from the sconces on the wall. She'd jumped in through the now broken window and seemed unafraid of the lethal group who faced her with claws and fangs unsheathed.

Amazing.

It wasn't the fact she wielded two guns in her small hands, or that she had one aimed directly at his balls that stilled him. It was her eyes. Golden hazel and glowing with anger, and maybe something more. Human or not, she'd found them, and that was a problem. The Guardians were secretive even amongst their own. A human should not have found them.

"Margo, what the hell are you doing?" Logan yelled at the female.

Anger roused, Egros turned on the male, but then understanding dawned. The normal had said *brother*. Logan was her brother.

Bloody hell.

Egros' gaze flitted between them, somehow, yes, they were related. Everyone was yelling and talking over one another, but the moment it was decided she was alone and wouldn't be killing anyone, most of the others left.

Only Elena, Logan, and Egros remained with the stranger. Well, stranger to him.

"You don't understand," Margo said, her untrusting gaze flitting between Elena and himself. "They've got you brainwashed, or under a spell, or just something!"

"That is ridiculous. I told you we are mates," Elena growled, and Egros knew the Panther was holding on by a thread.

"How do you even know about Shifters?" Elena snarled.

"The United States government knows about a lot of things. I happen to work for an agency that has been tracking Shifters for some time."

"What? Don't tell me you're with one of those military crews that hires Shifters to take out rival governments."

"What? Um, no," Margo replied, cocking her head to the side in a way that was way too endearing.

"Logan, I don't know what you are thinking, but your pink haired girlfriend is not human."

"Firstly," Egros cut in. "She is not his girlfriend. Elena is Logan's mate. Their bond is unbreakable. Secondly, Shifters do not cast spells. That would be impossible. Of everything you are bound to see and hear in this place, I assure you there is nothing untoward happening between your brother and Elena."

"Untoward? Really? And just who the fuck are you, Mr. Darcy?" she asked, her wickedly beautiful eyes narrowing at him.

For the first time in his life, Egros was about to tell a normal the truth about himself. He was not particularly worried, and that alone should have been a red flag. But his mouth was opening before he could overthink it.

I can always magic her later.

"My name is Egros Pyke, and I am a Witch."

Chapter Five

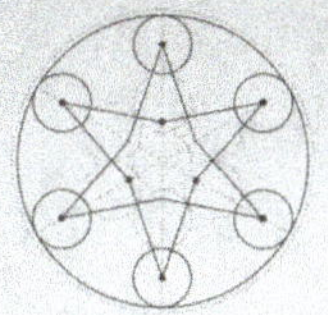

"**I** *am a Witch*."

The sound of his voice revealing that one phrase was on constant replay inside her mind. First, he was a dude. Not that she was sexist, but she sort of thought Witches were chicks with pointy hats or sparkly wands. Egros Pyke had neither.

After a few days in the mansion they all called the Keep, the man did not seem inclined to develop those things she'd always deemed witchy, either. He refused to reveal any proof that he could perform magic, assuming he had any.

In fact, the damned man deflected every inquiry she made about his supposed declaration that he was a Witch and any powers he might have right back at her. He was clever. Infuriating, but clever. And no, she was not disappointed. *Much.*

Four days had passed since Margo Wells had busted through the window of this old mansion that everyone who lived there called the Keep. The window had been seamlessly repaired, and no one seemed to hold it against her.

But still. Four days, and Margo had not managed a meeting with the leader of the cultish group of weirdos that had kidnapped her brother. She'd been interviewed over and over again by the man in front of her. For some reason, he could not get it through his thick skull that she was there to rescue her brother Logan.

He wanted to know about some group called the Loyalists. She'd come across the name infrequently, but it wasn't her department. Still, he seemed pretty convinced they had somehow brainwashed her to do their dirty work.

Whatever.

She was there for Logan, whether or not he believed her. He stared at her for a moment, jotted something down in his infernal notebook, then stared some more.

Well, if he thought she was going to whimper or

beg, he had another think coming. She was Margo Wells, DPCA Agent, marine, and lawyer.

So, she calmly stared back at the man, *er*, Witch. He didn't seem nervous or afraid, despite the fact she knew exactly what they were.

"She knows what we are, man," the one named Furio growled at Egros.

"Some normals do at some level. At any rate," Egros replied, easily.

They were seated in the dining room, and Margo was getting impatient. Hell. She had been impatient since day one. The events following her busting in on them replayed through her eidetic mind.

"Who named you Egros?"

"My father."

"Hmm." She'd pursed her lips.

"Must be a real dick to name his kid that."

"Indeed, he was." Egros had replied.

The man looked like he was fighting his grin. The large clock against the wall ticked away the minutes, but neither of them broke eye contact. It was a test of some sort, she was sure. But whether of strength or wills, she did not know. Besides, Margo did not want to look away.

He was fascinating. There was something about

him that drew him. Her blood raced inside of her, and her heartbeat seemed deafening even to her ears.

Her head started to spin, and visions came flooding in. It was difficult to sort them. That had never happened to her before. Almost as if they were conscious and aware on their own, wanting to show her all the possibilities.

Curious.

"Um, okay," Elena, her brother's psycho girlfriend had butted in, and Egros seemed startled to notice the female Shifter standing there.

"You got this, Egros?" she asked.

"Yes," he replied with a certainty Margo was not sure he actually felt.

"I think we can manage."

"Okay. Um, I don't want to bother him, but I'm going to go let Kingston know what's going on," Elena replied.

"Certainly," he agreed.

The female was all snarls and growls, but Margo was used to that. Shifters were something she'd seen before, though never a Dragon or Stallion. Witches, though, she was mighty curious about them.

"Is he going to see me today?" she asked before the male Witch could fall off into one of his many long silences.

*** * ***

Egros looked down. He knew she was right, but he wasn't exactly in a position to make demands. The Alpha should be here, interviewing her.

Their visitor was not exactly welcome. But neither was she threatening them at the moment, which was a pretty nice change. Still, Margo Wells seemed to know much more about Shifters and supernaturals than any normal should.

Far too much.

Protecting the supernatural world and keeping it hidden fell under the Guardians' purview. He needed to investigate just what she knew and how she found them. It wasn't like the Keep was on a bloody map.

Elena remained standing there. She watched the byplay between her new sister-in-law and Egros, eyebrows raised. He had the distinct feeling she was laughing at him.

"Uh, so you need any help before I go?" Elena asked.

"Of course not," Egros replied. "Ms. Wells and I were just chatting."

He kept her gaze, eyes never wandering from the

woman in question. She fascinated him. No doubt about it. And yet her very presence created a huge problem for the Guardians. A problem that had Elena and the others worried.

"Chatting, are we?" Margo said, leaning forward with her elbows on the table.

He must have done something right somewhere, because only the gods themselves could have given him the will to not glance down at the abundance of cleavage on display. Was she teasing him on purpose? He had to wonder.

"There's more to it, Eg," she crooned. "Don't you agree? More than just chatter between us."

Oh yeah.

The female was definitely playing with him. So Egros did look down, and after two very long seconds, flicked his gaze back to her glittering hazel eyes.

"I would think that an accurate assessment, Ms. Wells."

Margo gritted her teeth. He could practically hear the steam coming from her ears. She was pretty when she was angry, he noted with pleasure.

"Okayyy," Elena said, eyes bouncing back and forth between them like she was watching a tennis match.

If she was going to try to use her extremely hot body and pretty face to get answers, Egros was not going to deny her the victory of him being distracted. She was gorgeous, and he liked looking at her. Liked the way Margo's eyes tilted slightly at the corners, her curved eyelashes outlining them in thick black fringes. Her brows were naturally thin and arched.

Very pretty, he mused, shocking himself with that description. Egros was always the consummate professional. His sex life was low on the list of priorities. Like eating. When he was working, he could go for days without food. As it was, he'd been without a woman for months now.

"Did you just call me an *egg*?" His head whipped back to her face, confident he'd misheard the inept descriptor. Still, it wouldn't hurt to be sure, he figured.

"No, I called you *Eg* with one g."

"Right." Egros cleared his throat. "I don't know if that is any better---"

"Listen up Eg, whatever it is we are doing here, I don't think we can put it in the same category as two old biddies sipping tea on a Tuesday afternoon, do you?"

"Um---"

"Look, I know there is something up with you

guys. I have seen the claws on some of you, after all. And the agency I work for has come across chatter about the Guardians. That's you, right?"

"What else do you know?"

"Not much. The *DPCA* is what we like to call an intelligence gathering agency. We've been watching and collecting information on Shifters, Wolves, and Bears, because that was all we were aware of. Till now."

Shocked speechless, he merely waited for whatever she was gonna say next.

"So when I saw, we have more things going on between us, I mean, we have more things going on between us. Do you agree?"

"Indeed, Ms. Wells."

"Glad we understand each other," Margo said, and stood.

"Now look, I drove six hours to get here, and I have been waiting four days to talk to your leader or whatever the hell you call him."

"I apologize for the delay, it cannot be helped."

"Yeah, I figured you'd say that. But I am damn tired of waiting in this room."

"Ms. Wells, I'd like to talk more about the DP---"

"Department for Paranormal Creatures and Activity, Eg. We've been aware of you for some time.

But I admit, proving the existence of paranormal creatures beyond Wolves and Bears, like Witches for example, is definitely going to be good for my career."

"You can't do that!"

"See, and that's why of all these guys sitting here with their women, you are alone. Strong women don't like when men tell them what to do, Eg."

"What? I don't see what that has to do with anything. This is very serious, and we need to talk about it," Egros grumbled.

"Don't get uptight, Eg. You're a good looking guy. You just need to lighten up," she replied, and winked.

"Now, I am through here until I speak to the big guy," she said, and turned away from Egros.

"Hey, Logan?" Margo shouted at her brother.

"Yeah, Gogo?"

"What's there to do around here?" Margo asked.

"Well, you wanna check out my lab? I can show you what I am working on, then we can..."

The woman was an enigma. She stood up, dismissing Egros without so much as a backwards glance. And dammit, he wasn't done with his interviews. He needed to have something to present to his

Alpha, but the confounded woman would not sit still long enough.

She'd been vague in her answers, withheld more than her share of info, and seemed to not notice when he'd tried a simple compulsion charm. His magic was definitely wonky. Especially when it came to her!

"Blasted," Egros muttered, shuffling his notes in a pile.

"What has you cursing?" Byram asked, walking out of the shadows in that way the Vampire had about him.

Egros was used to it by now, so he was not startled. But he could see why people, even supes, thought the bloodsuckers creepy.

"Margo Wells is infuriating."

"I see, why not just bespell her then and be gone with the normal?"

"You don't think I tried? She is a human, Byram, you of all people should understand their frail natures. If I mess up a spell, it could damage her permanently."

A thought that had his power raging through his blood. Egros shook his head. It was no good. He would have to make a potion. Yes. That should work.

Anything else was simply too dangerous, and he was not about to risk the woman.

"I said," Byram repeated. "Why not use something stronger?"

"Because," Egros said, and refused to explain.

Yes, he was being childish, but what could he say? The thought of harm coming to the curly haired vixen was simply too much for him to take. No, that would not do.

Not at all.

Chapter Six

Egros sat at his desk in the room he'd always thought of as his potions' room. The Keep had always seemed able to oblige the inhabitants with whatever they needed, but who knew a conpar's needs would surpass a Guardian's?

He snarled and pushed the blasted science geek lab stuff out of his way. Okay, fine. He was being a brat, and he knew it.

Ever since Logan had moved his equipment into what was once Egros' space, and for a damn good reason too, he'd been feeling out of sorts. Was he even needed anymore? The human scientist had found a much better solution for stemming female Shifters' heat cycles than he or any other Witch ever had luck with.

Maybe the Guardians would be better off with him as their alchemist? Fuck. Now he was being ridiculous.

Logan was a genius, yes, but Egros was a Witch. The room was now set up so they could more easily work together, and really, it was fine. So what if it was like a Hogwarts meets tech geek science lab?

Whatever.

As long as he could work, he was fine. Besides, Egros enjoyed working with Logan. He'd been disappearing into his many projects for years when the outside world got too tough.

Focus was his friend.

Egros grimaced as he added the wrong ingredient to the batch of healing ointment he was making.

Damn it.

What was going on? He knew better than to add dried fire ants to his salve. That would cause more pain to whatever injury he was tempting to heal. Elementary stuff, and he knew better. For the first time since ever, at least, since he could recall, Egros' mind kept wandering away from the task at hand.

Where was his head?

As if he didn't know, he thought with a distinct

growl. He shook his head, hearing his mother's sweet voice echo in his brain from long ago.

"Witches do not growl, my son."

But he did, at least when he was a child and he used to play at being a Wolf or Tiger. Now, he supposed he did it out of habit. The byproduct of living with Shifters for so long, he supposed.

The reason he could not focus was, of course, the woman. One tiny human female had him making mistakes he would not have done in Witch school. Margo Wells should have been of no consequence to Egros Pyke, Witch and Guardian of Chaos.

He'd always been able to push all distractions out of his head when he was working. And yet, his brain was simply not cooperating. How was he supposed to commune with his powers with all these confounded images playing over and over again in his brain?

Only a handful of days and interactions with the vivacious normal, and Egros was reduced to this! Frustration runneth his cup over or whatever the fuck the saying was. He closed his eyes, willing himself to get back to work, but it was no good.

Her image remained firmly imprinted inside his brain. She was so different from anyone he'd ever known. Her glossy curls were at least ten different hues of brown, from the deepest mahogany to the brightest gold. They surrounded her head like some tawny halo, perfectly complementing her golden brown skin.

Did he mention how smooth and clear that skin seemed? Her face, obviously carved by angels, Egros had to stop himself from reaching out to touch her one time too many. He'd never been the type of man to just assume he had rights over a woman's person, and yet he was having a difficult time keeping his hands to himself.

She was just so, so, --- everything. She was so everything. Curvy and petite, with a wry wit and a ready laugh when something struck her as amusing. She'd answered their questions without telling them a thing more than she wanted to. Her secrets confounded him, her scent intoxicated him, and her hazel eyes hypnotized him.

The fact Margo Wells was completely comfortable amongst a group of Guardians amazed Egros. She was not scared or hostile. She was calm, cool, collected, and utterly attractive. And he was completely fucked.

Egros was responsible for causing serious discomfort to her only brother. A trespass she would surely never forgive. And could he blame her?

Not really, no.

But regardless of his feelings, he could own up to the truth. As far as he saw it the truth was this. Margo Wells was perfection.

Or as Fergie would say, she was *bowchicka-wowow smokin' hot*. Egros grinned, thinking of Storm's rather blunt mate. The redhead had a penchant for high end shoes and could out cuss a sailor. But she'd grown on him, and Egros was glad for her company and insights.

Fergie would definitely approve of the tough as nails female as a prospective mate, but what the hell was he thinking? She would never consider the likes of him suitable. The thought pained him, but he steered his brain to what the other Guardians might be thinking.

Elena was a little less trusting of the full human, but since Margo was related to Elena's mate, she was willing to offer her protection. Egros assumed Elena would eventually warm towards the female. She was, after all, practically related to her.

Holley, still recovering from childbirth, would want to meet Margo forthwith. The Witch was always excited when newcomers came to the Keep, but after being bound within its walls for nearly three hundred years, Egros could not blame her.

Then there was Jessenia, the kitchen Witch, mated to Furio. Her talents had superseded all expectations, including Egros'. She was tougher than they'd thought as well, rushing in to rescue her mate when the Loyalists had captured him. Still, Egros could not imagine the kind Witch being anything other than welcoming to Logan's sister. If nothing else, Margo's fondness for Jess' shortbread cookies was bound to win her over.

What the hell was he doing sitting there thinking about all this? Why should Egros care how the others found Margo or if they'd welcomed her? It was not his business.

With a dissatisfied grumble, he looked down at his ruined potion. Having messed up again, he grimaced and tossed the ruined ingredients into the special wastebin designed specifically for magical refuse.

It was one of many inventions he'd patented with the Council of Covens and sold to other Witches in the specialty shops available only to supernaturals. Egros was a firm believer in sharing his gifts, but he was also practical.

Money was a necessary evil, even in the supernatural world. Of course, as the heir to the Pyke fortune, he had inherited plenty. But Egros would never touch his father's money.

The minute he'd come of age to inherit, he'd given as much of it as he could to the orphanage that had seen his fellow Guardian, Furio, through his rough childhood. He funded hospitals and clinics for paranormal creatures, and studies that could help their kind thrive in secret. Putting the Pyke fortune to good use was his way of making up for his father's horrible past.

All these years later, Egros had amassed a fortune ten times what his father had left with nothing other than his talent and wit. Money did not really matter to him. He had all he needed right there.

Besides, as a Guardian, he lived in the Keep. The *manetuwak* or spirits therein had always provided whatever it was he wanted or needed. Sometimes doing so before he'd asked for it. Something he greatly appreciated.

His rooms were furnished to his preference, as was his clothing, and the workrooms he used for potions and other casting. But even the Keep could do nothing to stop his mind from wandering back to *her*.

The air seemed thick with frustration. *His*. But

could anyone blame him? The woman was a total enigma. Her answers had been vague when questioned about why and how she'd come to the Keep. She'd smiled and zipped her lip, refusing to tell them anything more detailed until their leader, Kingston, was available. Of course, that did not stop the questions from filling his head.

Why was she there? Was it simply to get her brother? How had she found them?

All good questions that needed answers but contemplating those would not answer the question most on Egros' mind.

How would her lips feel pressed to mine?

Fuck. This was bad. He had no business thinking anything like that about Margo Wells. Normals were not allowed in the Keep, unless mated to one of the Guardians within. And far as he knew, Witches did not have fated mates.

Even if the thought pained him, it was only the truth. Margo was not his, and regardless of his attraction to her, she would have to go. Worry had him frowning as he thought of the extensive mind wiping process the female would have to endure.

After his failures at using simple charms on her, he knew this was the only other option, and yet, he hesitated. The human mind was a fragile thing, and one wrong move could turn a perfectly capable person into a vegetable.

Unacceptable.

His power thrummed and sizzled at the thought of any threat to the female. His chest reverberated with what sounded more and more distinctly like an animalistic growl.

He was being an idiot. How many times had he wished he was Wolf like Storm, or a Dragon like Kingston? Especially when he'd been younger. But he was a Witch, not a Shifter. And that wasn't too shabby a thing to be if he did say so himself.

There's more to it, Eg. Don't you agree?

Her words played back in his head. Once more, his chest rumbled, and his magic pulsed. Egros stilled. Physically, he was frozen in place, but his mind was moving at a hundred miles per hour.

Since when did his magic have opinions or feelings? Never. Not about any one person or thing. Certainly never about a woman.

He grabbed his computer. The thing was magically enhanced with spells as well as Draco Fortis security software for paranormal searches on *Ghoulgle*, the magical net for supernaturals. Nostradamus, an underground Ghoul, and his super fly girlfriend, Emily, had invented the search engine as the end all for information for magical beings.

Graves Enterprises was another solid structure in supernatural software development. They were the best in the business, far as he knew. Owned by one of the Macconwood Wolf Pack's Wolf Guard, Egros frowned and started thinking. Who would know more about this kind of thing than one of their mates?

Without hesitating, he sent an email off to Sherry Morgan-McAllister. The woman was the single most powerful Witch alive in the world today. The Morrigan walked the Earth once more, and if anyone would have the answers, it was her.

Of course, whether she would share them was another question entirely. Still, he had to try.

Grrr.

Chapter Seven

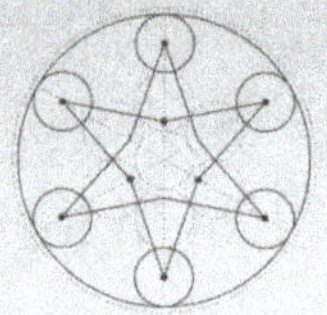

Margo took a bite from the still warm cinnamon bun that sat in a massive tray on the long table in the dining room. This place, *the Keep*, was incredible. The lights seemed to glow at the thought, and she bit back a grin. Incredible and apparently not above preening.

The last few days had been like a strange vacation of sorts. She'd eaten well, slept better, and spent some much needed brother and sister time with Logan. She'd also met and got to know his mate, Elena, a bit better.

After months of watching Shifters covertly for her job, being able to interact with them was quite thrilling. And boring. They were just like regular people, except they looked better, ate more, and had ridiculous amounts of energy.

Sighing, she was glad Logan had come to get her from her borrowed room to have breakfast. The food in this place was insanely good, and all due to Jessenia, one of the Shifter's mates.

So yeah, it was pleasant so far. Especially the glimpses she'd gotten of Egros. He'd confessed to being a Witch, and Margo's pulse had raced.

Still, she hadn't exactly seen him perform magic. Her hunt for proof that magic did in fact exist was so close to fruition, she could taste it. But if being evasive was a skill, he had that shit down cold.

"Let's talk about you being a Witch," she'd said *during one of their question and answer sessions.*

"I'd rather discuss you," he'd replied, *a cute grin on his face.*

"Can you do a trick for me? A magic trick?"

"I'm not a circus magician, Ms. Wells. I do not do tricks."

She'd obviously insulted him, but the look on his face was so worth it. His sometimes dark eyes had grown even darker, and she'd had to bite back her grin. He was entirely too tense. With the new legalization of certain recreational herbs, Margo wondered if he wouldn't perhaps benefit from a little herbal therapy. Not that she ever indulged. As a law enforcement agent, she was not allowed to partake. College her would be so pissed.

"So, how is it going?" Logan asked.

"Well, your guy here has questioned me time and again and I still haven't met the boss," she replied.

"yeah, sorry about that," Logan frowned. "Apparently, it's customary for his kind to stay in his caver, *er*, bedroom protecting his mate and newborn," Logan explained badly.

"I see, and will this caveman ever come out of the Dark Ages to speak to me, you think?"

Logan spit his coffee onto the table and glared at his sister. She handed him a napkin, smirking as she did. Margo never tired of frustrating him.

"Not funny, Gogo," Logan said, still coughing.

"You need to lighten up," she replied. "Tell me, which one of you replaced the window? It is seamless," she noted.

Her eyes had wandered to the window where she'd busted through a few nights ago. She stared, amazed that there was no evidence of her entrance at all. Even if they were handy, she doubted anything other than magic could have cleared that up without even a drop of spackle or glue residue. Sure, they could simply be talented at construction and home repairs, but she doubted it.

Yeah. Right.

If her work with the DPCA had taught her anything, it was that things were never what they seemed. The secret government agency had been aware of the existence of Werewolves and Shifters for some time, though they were somewhat limited in their knowledge.

Notoriously private, paranormal beings sometimes worked with the human government on the dl. Margo would have killed to be in on those assignments.

Alas, she was relegated to the legal department after an incident in the field that had left too many dead and more wounded. Due to an NDA, she was not permitted to talk about that now. To this day, she found peace in knowing her actions during that skirmish had saved tens of thousands.

And her family thought she was some bleeding heart lawyer who traveled the world to help those less fortunate. Ha! Even her brother had believed that lie until now.

"What?" Logan asked, helping himself to more coffee.

"How long have you known?" she asked without any buildup.

All these years, they'd never directly lied to each other. Omissions, certainly. Both their jobs had called for that sort of thing. Logan had worked for companies involving top secret pharmaceutical formulas he was not privileged to discuss. And she worked for the government, enough said. So, yeah, without preamble, she asked him flat out the one question that had been on her mind the last few days. How long had he known about the paranormal world? She waited, shaking her head when his brow creased.

"Don't tell me any stories, Logan. How long have you known?" Margo asked again. She believed in getting straight to the point.

"That you're scary without coffee? Most of our lives, Gogo," he replied, using the nickname she hated.

"Most of our lives," he reiterated, and offered her a refill of what turned out to be truly excellent coffee.

She mock glared at him, but didn't bother replying. Instead, Margo took a healthy swig of the piping hot stuff.

Mmm. Now that was good coffee.

Eyes closed as she indulged in a second swallow,

Margo felt the hairs on the back of her neck rise as someone else entered the room. It was *him*. The man she'd dubbed Eg. The only male Witch she had ever heard of.

Somehow, she just felt it whenever he entered a room. It was unnerving and exciting at the same time. Not that Margo would ever admit she liked it when she felt his broody eyes on her almost as surely as she'd imagined his hands. Another thing she wasn't rushing to tell anyone.

Okay, fine. Since the second after she'd crashed through the enormous picture window and her eyes found the tall, dark haired man standing protectively in front of her brother, her curiosity had been piqued.

She'd spied Logan and Elena, whom she'd admittedly referred to as the *cult skank* before she'd officially met her and had taken no notice of the others. Just their heat signatures. Certain she'd had enough of the specialty Shifter strength rounds in her guns. Margo had busted into the Keep determined to save her brother.

Only, Logan didn't want to be saved. He was quite happy. More so than she had ever seen him. It was not that difficult a concept, but Margo had to admit she'd been surprised to see her bro so in love.

In love and claimed by a Panther Shifter who'd defend him to the death. And that was the only reason Margo didn't push the issue.

The Guardians, or whatever these people called themselves, seemed to her like a group of mercenary soldiers fighting the good fight, but not exactly getting paid. Their mission was unclear, but she was damn sure her boss would want to know. That had been her first mistake. Trying to send a text off to Mother in front of him, Egros Pyke, the self-identified male Witch, had led to the confiscation of the phone and other equipment.

They allowed her to keep her foldable knife, so she'd feel safe. Apparently, they weren't worried about that particular skill set. More fool them.

Elena walked in, and before she greeted anyone else, she bent to kiss Logan lovingly on the lips. Something whispered between them had Logan's cheeks turning a dusky shade of red, while Elena's eyes sparkled in a matching hue.

Who knew her fathead brother could be so happy? Margo swallowed back a sob of joy that threatened to burst from her lips. She was thrilled for him, at the same time her heart broke a little.

They'd always done everything together. Their first time riding bikes without training wheels was with one another. They'd taken their first SATs together. Hell, they'd even gotten stitches for the first time with each other. Ironically, that was on the same day they'd learned to ride their bikes.

Oh Logan, I am so happy for you, she thought, and meant it.

If only she could stop the ache inside her chest from spreading.

Chapter Eight

Margo watched the exchange unashamedly. Their love was obvious, sweet, and tender. Still in that ever hopeful, blooming springtime stage. Much like the weather outside.

New Jersey was notorious for inconstant weather in the months of April, May, and June. But every day was a promise of something warm and wonderful, and she saw the same promise in her brother's eyes when he looked at his mate.

Great. She was happy for him. No, really, she was. Even if his happiness seemed to highlight Margo's own perpetually single state. Once that thought had entered her brain, Margo could only see one solution. He was tall, thin, with a swimmer's build and a look of careful consideration on his handsome face every time she'd seen him.

Egros Pyke was what her Auntie Beth had always referred to as a tall drink of water on a hot summer's day. She'd never known what the old woman had been talking about, till now.

Dayum.

Now, where had that thought come from? Sure, it had been a hot minute since Margo had indulged in a little *somethin' somethin'*, but since when did she find skinny, tall, goth looking dudes hot?

Since now.

She hated it when she argued with herself. But *inner frisky her* did have a point. The man seemed to exude a mysterious sexiness that she was dying to explore.

Okay, so on further perusal, Margo admitted he wasn't rocking a full on goth vibe. He did wear a lot of black, though. And that inky dark hair of his fell all the way to his chin in front, like some 90s alt-rock star. Still, Eg seemed unintentionally indifferent to his appearance.

People worked so hard to look cool, but Egros Pyke did it without even trying. He looked like one of the front men she'd hung posters of all over her college dorm room. That was the stuff she and

Logan used to listen to back when they were in their teens.

Fine. Big bad secret agent that she was, Margo still had a weakness for brooding bad boys. And dayum, but this guy looked just like that actor who played Loki in the latest Hollywood production of super-heroism.

Margo was a sucker for good old fashioned comic book universe action flicks. Especially the ones that featured smexy bad guys with dark good looks and all that intensity.

Ooh. Gave her shivers.

Snap out of it, she scolded herself.

Margo was too dang old for this. She was a grown woman, and she could damn well control her carnal appetites. Squirming in her seat a little, she purposely ignored Eg's entrance. Now was not the time to drool over any man, *or* Witch, for that matter.

"Morning, Egros," Logan said, bringing the man directly over to where brother and sister had been chatting.

Fucking great. Thank you very much, she thought angrily at her genius idiot brother.

"Good morning, Logan, Ms. Wells," Egros returned, inclining his head slightly.

"Please, join us," Logan said, engaging the man

in a conversation about formulas that went way over Margo's head.

Good, that would give her a second to breathe and collect herself. Their conversation sounded like background noise, and that was fine to Margo. Smart as she was, she had no patience for science. Give her something to investigate, a case to argue, and she was all over that like bees on honey.

But that wasn't the issue. It was the scent of mint and fresh rosemary that seemed to be coming from him, driving her nuts. She wanted to get closer, bury her nose in the crook of his neck and just breathe him in.

"Excuse us, Ms. Wells," Egros murmured, startling her with his deep voice. "Um, we can talk shop a bit later, Logan. I don't think your sister is all that interested."

"My sister? Oh, sorry, Gogo, forgot you were there." Logan grinned and stuffed another bite of cinnamon bun in his big, dumb mouth.

He did not just call her that. Ugh! *Inner frisky Margo* turned into *inner seething Margo* on a second's notice. She was ready to scratch her brother's eyes out for the slip.

Dumb fathead.

She hadn't called Logan, and his abnormally

large skull, that since they were little. Even thinking it now made her giggle a bit at the naughty thought. Auntie Beth would not like that one bit. She'd been more mom to Margo than her actual mother, and had taught her kindness was, in fact, a virtue.

One she was in short supply of at the moment. Especially where her big-mouthed brother was concerned.

"Gogo?" Egros inquired.

Great. Margo glared at her bro. The idiot did not even realize he was making her uncomfortable, did he? That was the thing about being a fathead. Logan was usually pretty oblivious about stuff that was common sense for others.

"An unfortunate nickname from when I was a kid," she reluctantly explained.

"Really?"

"Yeah," Logan added, unhelpfully. "She was always so impatient. No matter where we were off to, it was always *'Go, Logan go!'* So I shortened it to Gogo whenever we were hanging out."

"I see. So you didn't grow up in the same household?"

"Duh," she snarled. "Don't you have something to do? More inane questions to ask me?"

"Gogo!" Logan admonished, but she was so done with him.

"Ah, still impatient?" Egros asked, and dammit, the man smirked. Not unkindly, but still.

"Only when I'm being *handled.*"

"Well then, we'll have to make sure not to let that happen."

"You're damn straight," she replied, and bit into her pastry with relish.

Chatter around the table was friendly, but Margo sensed everyone was waiting. She noticed the seat at the head of the table was still empty. How long did a man have to spend alone with his newborn and wife, for fuck's sake? Didn't he know she was there?

The DPCA would kill for the information she was secretly stockpiling inside her photographic memory. Shifters, Witches, *magic.* All of it was real. Not just what the government agency had told her, but so much more.

If she could just somehow bring back proof of this place and its inhabitants. Maybe even arrange for a meeting between Mother and the one called Kingston Baldric. Then she would finally be vindicated.

Tired of being laughed at behind her back for

her belief that there was more out there than some Wolves and Bears. But Margo was right. There was. She just had to figure out how she was going to prove it to her boss.

"So," she said, deciding to cut the shit. "How many of you are Shifters? What kind of animal do you turn into? And how many of you here are Witches? And are *you* really a *Witch*? Wouldn't you be like a Warlock or a Wizard?" she asked, pointing at Egros.

"Uh---"

"Well---"

"You see---"

"Margo!" hissed Logan.

"What?"

"That isn't polite, and you know it." Logan frowned.

"That's not polite? These folks can turn into beasts that can rip our faces off before we can blink, and you think I am being impolite by asking them to explain what they are?"

"Margo," Logan growled.

"I want answers, Logan. It's been days and all we've done is eat. The food was delicious, but I'm not gonna forget my questions because of a couple dozen cookies. And you know me, brother. I won't stop pushing until I get what I want."

"Can't you just stop being an agent for one minute," he grumbled, tossing his hands in the air.

"Excuse me," Egros said. "If I may interrupt?"

"Go ahead," she said, narrowing her eyes at the man.

"I apologize, Ms. Wells. You must have many questions. As do we. You haven't answered our inquiries, and yet you demand we answer yours---"

"I did not demand. Not yet," she replied, and crossed her arms over her chest.

She hated when people pointed out the flaws in her logic. Besides, there were things she simply couldn't answer. These people didn't have the clearance necessary to hear it.

"Pardon me, then, for that misrepresentation. But you must understand we have the right to protect our secrets---"

"Why? Why do you have that right? I have a right to know who and what you are. For all I know, you are keeping my brother hostage!"

"I think we both know, that is not true."

"Look," Logan butted in. "We should wait for Kingston---"

"Shut up," Margo growled at her brother.

"Yeah, Logan, perhaps you should be quiet," Eg added.

"Don't tell my brother what to do or I'll---" she snapped at the wickedly handsome Witch.

"Or you'll what?"

Egros was now standing toe to toe with Margo. She was so mad, she was growling. His eyes were flashing like purple lightning at her. She felt the hair on the back of her neck stand up. It felt like little shivers of electricity were dancing all over her, tickling her skin. They were both breathing heavily, and Margo swore she could taste his rosemary mint scent.

It was delicious. Egros blinked, his eyes zeroing in on her mouth, and Margo swayed a little on her feet. The noise surrounding them fell away, and all she could do was stare at his lips. Need and arousal warred within her, but before she could do anything stupid, like throw herself at him, a very large someone cleared his throat from right next to them.

Chapter Nine

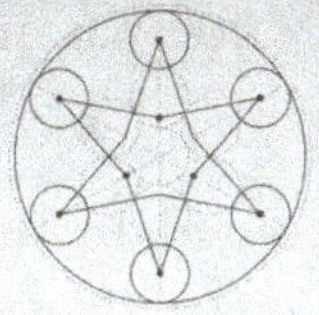

Egros was two seconds away from plastering his face to hers in front of all and sundry.

Thank the gods for Kingston. His arrival was just in time. At best, the tiny female would have planted the knife she kept in her back pocket somewhere between his third and fourth rib as he had no doubt she could with unerring accuracy. At worst, she'd kiss him back.

That end would only serve to destroy Egros' life as he knew it. Somehow, he'd subconsciously accepted that as fact. Kissing Margo Wells would change everything.

But was that a risk he was willing to take?

His magic swirled and gathered deep inside of him. Rising up from that place in the pit of his stomach, all the way to his chest. It beat there, pulsing in time with his heart. For a brief moment, her eyes glittered, and he wondered if she would be the one to break this spell. Perhaps she'd take the decision right out of his hands.

Excitement and anticipation buzzed along his skin, his magic racing along with it. Egros had never felt so alive, so enthralled by a female. Never like this, never before, and he'd stake his life on never after, as well.

"Well! Looks like I've arrived in time," the Diamond Dragon announced.

He walked around them, further into the room, with the air of an Alpha Dragon Shifter. Kingston had every reason to be supremely confident, not only in his position as their leader, but in his life.

Of course, Egros knew of the man's inner demons and struggles, and he could not be happier for Kingston than he was now. A closer look at his friend and Alpha revealed Kingston most likely had not slept a lot the past few days. And yet, he seemed infinitely content with his lot in life.

Unlike this currently sweating and agitated Witch. The lucky bastard.

Egros thought unkindly. He cleared his throat and pushed away his annoyance. With a slight bow of his head in the Dragon's direction, Egros stepped back from the tempting female.

Of course, Kingston Baldric, ever the Alpha, took in the situation with keen eyes. He tilted his head slightly, and Egros knew he was asking him a question. One he did not dare consider. So, the Witch ignored it, keeping his eyes frontward.

"So," the Dragon said, sitting down at the head of the table. "You are our Logan's sister."

"Yes, Logan is *my* brother," Margo replied, seeming to correct the Alpha's use of the possessive *our*.

"I see," Kingston growled, one eyebrow raised.

Shit. Not many people dared hold the man's stare, but the little vixen was doing just that. Egros' magic stirred. Not at all happy with the way the Dragon was openly glaring at the female.

Though, to be honest, Egros was quite shocked, and for some strange reason, proud that she could hold the enormous man's stare so long. Finally, and to his relief, Margo averted her gaze with an angry puff of breath.

That made Egros grin. She was gutsy for a human. He'd give her that. But she was also prudent. A lifesaving virtue if ever there was one.

"How did you find us?" Kingston asked.

The Dragon did not believe in dilly dallying and chose to speak directly. Egros waited for her reply, curious as to her response. In all their interactions, it was the one she'd most vehemently refused to answer. Margo exhaled heavily. He already knew she had no desire to confess her methods.

Now, seeing that expression on her lovely face made Egros even more curious. He turned, taking a closer look. They'd both reseated themselves at Kingston's insistence, and he found the damn chair constraining as he waited. She tapped the table with her short, polished fingernails, and her hazel eyes flitted to her brother.

Was that Guilt? But why?

"Fine," she grunted. "I micro-chipped Logan."

"You did what?!" her brother shouted in outrage.

He'd stood up so swiftly, the chair he had been sitting on crashed to the stone floor. Margo's only moved back as she also stood, going toe to toe with her taller brother.

"Don't take that tone with me, *fathead*," she retorted.

It was amazing how much they looked alike. Skin and hair colors so vastly different, and yet their hazel eyes blazed with passion as they took identical stances against the other.

"I might have always been on the run as a kid, but you were the one always getting into trouble. I did it so I could protect you---"

"Protect me from what? I am a grown man---"

"Who was abducted by Shifters! Dangerous man eating Shifters!"

"Um, we don't eat humans," Storm said.

"Actually, I'm a vegetarian," Furio added unhelpfully.

"Shut up!" Logan and Margo screamed at the same time.

"Hold on, everyone, please just a minute now," Egros stood up, getting between Elena and Margo, who were staring each other down again.

"*Ohmygawd!* You guys! What the hell? I was napping," an angry, and very pregnant, Fergie came walking into the room in her custom Ferragamo slippers.

How she got the design house to create them for her, he did not know, or care, for that matter. Egros had other things to worry about. Besides, Storm probably procured them, and the Wolf certainly had his methods.

"Butt out, Egros," snapped Logan.

"Stop telling everyone what to do, Logan," Margo snapped.

Was she defending him now? Egros wondered. And was it perverse he felt happiness at the very idea the beautiful Margo had stood up for him to her own brother?

Fuck. Yes. It totally was. Pathetic, Egros. Very pathetic.

He rubbed a hand over his face as everyone resumed their shouting and talking over the other. It was a goddamned disaster, and Egros' magic was starting to zap at him anxiously.

"Quiet!" Kingston roared. "Now, we are all going to sit down here and discuss this rationally."

"Fine, but first someone needs to dig that microchip out of my ass!" Logan bellowed.

That particular announcement was followed by a unanimous round of *not its* from the entire group. Egros included.

Much as he still felt he had a lot to make it up to both Elena and Logan, he was not digging in that guy's ass cheeks for a damn thing.

Nope. No fucking thank you.

"Um, yeah. Okay, so Logan? We can figure that part out later. Now, I have a mate and newborn Dragonling to get back to---"

"Dragonling? OMG! You really turn into a Drag-on?" Margo gasped, and Kingston closed his eyes.

The Alpha more than likely did not mean to reveal anything about himself. But the cat was pretty much out of the bag, and there were only two ways this could go. One, they enlightened their fellow Guardian's sister-in-law as to the actual facts about the world. Or two, they erased her memory.

Both he and his magic were in favor of the former. Suddenly, he felt the most absurd need to protect the little vixen, to keep her from harm at all costs. As if she needed him to, he thought disgusted with himself.

"Egros," Kingston said, his eyes white with his beast. "Take Margo to your office."

Fuck.

He knew what those words meant, and everything inside of him raged against it. Still, Egros could not disobey a direct order.

Much as he wanted to. Shit. He was going to have to erase everything that had happened in the past few days, the Keep, the supernatural world she'd recently uncovered, not to mention *himself*, from Margo's memory.

What fresh fucking hell was this day turning into?

"Egros?"

"Yes," he replied to the Dragon.

"Come find me when you are done."

He nodded, too angry for words.

Margo was arguing with her brother, and Elena was trying to get his attention. The Panther Shifter had picked up on what their Alpha had ordered Egros to do. It was up to her to break the news to her mate.

Not an easy job, for sure. But Egros' was worse. He'd formed some sort of attachment to the woman, despite they'd only spoken less than a dozen times.

Remember your vows and focus, he told himself. But that didn't make him feel any better.

"Come with me, Ms. Wells."

Then he turned and walked away. She was curious and would follow him to his workroom. Once there, he'd perform a forgetting ritual. With any luck, that would suffice.

But when had Egros ever been lucky?

Chapter Ten

The Witch walked around her in a slow, yet perfect circle. It felt decadent and naughty, calling him that. She didn't know why. It was simply who he was.

A Witch.

But she could almost imagine his power reaching out across the void, calling to her in a seductive song. Foolish nonsense, but Margo always had an active imagination.

Whatever magic was, she was too new to it to have any understanding of its capabilities. But damn, she was giddy with the high of being right.

All the naysayers and those who'd looked at her like she was crazy could suck it! Ha! Magic was real, or at least, it seemed that way. She'd never been so happy, but she still needed proof. And with a little maneuvering, this guy was going to give it to her.

She looked around the room and frowned. No windows, no doors except the one they'd come in from. It was dark and depressing. Boring too with shelf after shelf of books, and all sorts of geeky equipment that could only belong to Logan.

Her brother was an odd one. Brilliant, but odd. Anyway, this place was not at all what she'd imagined a Witch's lair to look like.

She snorted at the word *lair* as it popped into her head. Eg turned and raised an eyebrow inquiringly. But Margo ignored the question and looked, really looked, at him.

Shaking her head, she took in his stiff shoulders, and constant frown. His hair fell across his forehead as he shrugged, then went back to gathering notes and vials. Margo wasn't precisely sure what was about to happen, but that pesky inner sight of hers was on full alert.

Something was going down. Something she wasn't too sure she was going to like. Eg's agitation was getting to her. Before she could stop herself, or question her own actions, Margo placed her hand on top of his.

"Okay. Stop banging things and look at me," she commanded.

"What? Um, why?"

"Just do it," she said, and waited for him to comply.

His fingers wrapped around hers, and she was stunned to discover it felt good, holding hands in the dark crowded room.

"What's going on, Eg?" she asked, using the nickname she hadn't bothered to ask permission for.

"What did the Dragon tell you to do?" she added.

Margo was far from stupid. Her foresight was a curse sometimes, but in her line of work, she'd learned more often than not, it was its own reward. She braced herself, waiting for the moment he would come clean.

Finally, she gazed into Egros' shamrock green eyes. Green, huh? She mused. She could have sworn they'd been blue, or violet, maybe even brown before. Whatever the color, his eyes sure were pretty. They glittered in the darkness, bright with resolve to tell the truth as they stared into hers. Or maybe she imagined that.

No. Not imagined.

That extra sense she sometimes loved, sometimes

hated, told her he meant to be truthful. The pull she felt growing so powerful between them, he felt it too. She was certain of it. Well, in that moment she was, anyway.

In all honesty, this place, the people in it, all of it combined, was like some crazy fantasy. Something she'd imagined or saw on TV. A make-believe playground for grown-ups that she'd read in a book, maybe.

But what author would bother making up such a place? And in New Jersey too. Ha! That was laughable. The Garden State wasn't known for hidden mansions in forest paradises, and that was exactly what she'd thought of this place when she spied it several nights ago. Among the pines and beeches, black walnuts, and more in the Jersey pine barrens sat the Keep like a stone fortress amidst all the burgeoning green.

Of course, at the time, she hadn't thought much beyond finding her brother. Fathead he may be, he was hers, and she would always have his back. Now that she had found him, and knew he was safe and sound, Margo realized she hadn't planned the 'what next' part of this failed smash and grab job.

Egros knew, though. He knew, and he was about to tell her. That fact made her heart warm just a little bit more towards the too handsome Witch. From green to gold, his eyes changed, and she blinked to make sure she wasn't just seeing things.

What the what now?

"Margo," he said her name, and her attention flashed back to him. "Kingston told me to bring you here so that I might wipe your memory of this place and all you have learned since your arrival."

"What? Sonovabitch! That's not fair," she sputtered, angry beyond the capability of coherent speech.

"I didn't even learn anything besides the fact there were more than Bears and Wolves out there! I already knew about paranormals! The US government has a branch dedicated to studying you!"

"What?" he asked, confusion evident on his handsome face. "Explain, Margo. Please."

It was then she noticed he'd been using her first name. Their hands still entwined, she looked down at them, then pulled away. What was she doing? She shouldn't be attracted to him. Not here and not now.

"Look," she replied, closing her eyes and gathering her thoughts.

"The DPCA knows about Shifters. We aren't part of the military or the FBI or CIA, for that matter. We are something else. A top secret branch of government that has been aware of people, para-normals, who turn into Wolves and Bears for years now. Some have been tapped by other secret branches of the military and have done work for them, but not us. We've simply watched and gathered information," she began, barely making sense to herself, let alone the confused Witch sitting there.

"So, you're telling me you are in cahoots with a secret government agency that knows something, but not everything about the paranormal world?"

"Yes," she nodded. "We don't interfere, we simply collect information. And Egros, you can help me. I mean, you're a Witch. That means magic is real. And let me tell you something, I have been looking for a way to prove that for years. You can't take this away from me---"

"Who me? No. I told you, Kingston says you need to have your memory wiped. I am sorry, Margo, but---"

"Why does he get to decide?"

"He is our Alpha. You don't understand---"

"Then help me, Eg. Make me understand," she pleaded.

"Not for my job, but for me. I've, I've been seeing things my whole life. Images, snapshots, sometimes whole scenes playing out like video clips in my head.

My Auntie Beth thought I was crazy, had me locked up for a few months when I was a kid. Not even Logan knows," she whispered, wiping her face with her fingers.

She hated crying. Crying didn't fix anything. Only hard work and determination had ever helped Margo when the going got rough. That, and patience. Patience was another of those dang virtues she'd always strived for. Auntie Beth, God rest her soul, had given her a strong moral compass, like many good Christian women had. Her own mother had been absentee, which was likely for the best.

But without any other adults to take full custody of her, she'd learned to hide that truth about herself. And, God, how it hurt to have to do that! Without any prodding, Margo confessed to Egros about her sight, and the years she'd spent hiding it.

"Incredible," he whispered.

"Me? Nah. Crazy, maybe. I mean, it's not like I turn into a Wolf, or a Panther, like Elena."

"Me either," he said, offering her a tissue and a smile. "Actually, Shifters don't *turn into* Bears and Wolves, *they are* Bears and Wolves. And Dragons, Stallions, Panthers, and more, Margo, so much more than that."

"What more? Tell me, Eg. Teach me, please. I

will be a good student. I swear it."

Margo watched his eyes darken now to almost black, and she wanted to grin, knowing she had him. Men were so easy to figure out. She just had to smile and show some enthusiasm, and they followed her around like puppies. She tried not to let her disappointment show and was stunned by the fact she wanted him to be different.

Why should that even matter?

"Come on, Eg," she said, trying to shake off that bit of weirdness. "The world deserves to know the truth about all of you, your friends, and magic. If magic exists, it's only fair---"

"Stop right there," he said, shaking his head and she knew then that she lost him.

Even more compelling was why she should feel so relieved knowing she'd lost her only lead?

Margo had no time to contemplate her strange reactions to this man. No, not when he was talking again, and *surprise surprise*, she actually wanted to listen.

"The world is not fair. Never has been. And humans are among the most cruel, judgmental, and greedy beings out there."

"Hey!"

"Can you honestly say humans would react well

to the news their neighbors are actually dual natured creatures? Beings who can shift to different forms, *sometimes multiple different forms*, from animals to mythological creatures, and more than that. Would the average Joe or Marcus or Steve like hearing that their wives and daughters and sons live next door to thousand pound Bears or two ton dragons who can breathe fire? Shifters have the increased strength, speed, stealth, and deadly traits their wild cousins have only with the addition of cognitive reason. And I already said there are more than your regular zoological creatures from A to Zed. So, what then, eh, Margo?"

"I don't know what you want me to say."

"I want you to think, and be honest with yourself, then answer my question. Would the average human like knowing that supernaturals exist?"

Fuck. When he put it like that... ugh. Margo gritted her teeth. Anger and impotence cursed through her. Egros was right. She knew he was right. But after so many years of trying to understand her own precognitive abilities and working to prove magic actually existed. Beyond that which she'd recently found out at the DPCA, Margo wanted to show the world that magic was real. Was she just supposed to let all that go now?

Frustrated tears pricked her eyes, but she wouldn't give him the satisfaction of crying. She stared him down, willing her anger to simmer down. But it was no good. Margo was torn between wanting to scream and wanting to kiss him.

Damn the man for being so stinking good looking. The sympathy she saw filling his gaze, as if he regretted his harsh words, just wasn't fair. After all, he wasn't rude or wrong even. He was simply being honest with her. Margo respected honest.

"So, do all paranormal beings hate humans or just you?" she asked, trying to regain her composure.

"I hold no hatred in my heart for you or any human, Margo. This is not personal."

"It is to me," she replied, glaring.

"I was given a direct order by the leader of our group. I could not disobey him, even if I wanted to."

She huffed out a breath and walked to the farthest wall. It was made of some kind of stone and looked ancient and unbreakable. But she never was one to take things for what they seemed. Margo lifted a heavy iron pot and hit the thing, once, twice, allowing her rage to flow through her.

Egros just stood there, watching with concern heavy on his face. When she was utterly spent, she felt his arms come around her. He took the heavy iron pot and replaced it on the shelf. The damage she'd done to the wall began to smooth away and repair in front of her eyes. Margo stopped, stunned.

"How did you do that?"

"It's not me," he replied, gently. "The Keep is inhabited with *manetuwak,* magical spirits. They protect these walls, repair them, when need be, and see to our needs."

"Wow. That is pretty amazing," she mumbled.

"It is. Look, Margo," he began.

"Fine," she replied, cutting him off.

Margo turned and faced him. She wasn't afraid of the male Witch, but she was hurt by his words. Not so much the words themselves, but the truth behind them. It was irrational, and unreasonable, but she couldn't help it.

"Margo---"

"You're right, okay? Just leave it at that."

She stormed over to a chair and sat down heavily.

"Well? What are you waiting for?" she asked.

"What do you mean?"

"Let's get this over with."

Breathing unsteadily, she waited for him to make the next move.

Chapter Eleven

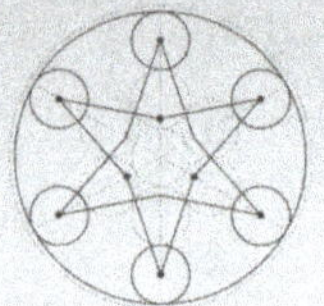

His green eyes darkened to amber, as if his own sadness affected the color. She blinked, sure she was seeing things, but no. From shamrock green, to black, to amber. Only a shimmer of that emerald color remained in the now honey-colored depths.

"Here," he said, stalking over to where she sat.

He picked up a tumbler of clear liquid, could have been water for all she knew, but it wasn't. Somehow, Margo knew that glass contained something that would take away her memories, clear her mind of this place, finding her brother, and *him*. The thought saddened her.

"Drink this," Eg said, getting a second vial ready.

Margo tossed it back, grimacing at the sharp, bitter taste as it slid down her throat. The next one he handed her was sweet and floral, like hyacinths on a warm spring day. The one after that was terrible, it tasted like water after a handful of dirty pennies had been left to soak for a month. She wiped her tongue on the tissue he handed her, not embarrassed in the least.

"Ugh, how many of these do I have to take?"

"That is all. Now, I need you to look into my eyes, Margo, and follow the direction."

Always a good pupil, she sat there silently and gazed into his then sky blue eyes. That was strange, wasn't it? His eyes didn't just get darker or lighter the way some did when a person was angry, or happy, or horny. They didn't change from blue green to green blue like her friend Doris' did depending on what color top she wore.

His eyes were a revolving door of colors. Each one vibrant and expressive. And hot. Did she mention hot? Margot squirmed in her seat as liquid pooled between her legs. The thought of Egros Pyke and his multicolored eyes left her feeling both needy and lusty.

Knock it off, she told herself, listening to the

sultry timbre of his voice. Eg held her gaze, asked her to relax, to trust him. Oddly enough, she did.

His blue eyes widened as he continued to speak, sparks of purple swimming in their depths. She was certain he was not even speaking English anymore. But that didn't matter because Margo was no longer listening to his words.

No, now she was floating down the river of her own consciousness. The water was warm and comforting, and the pull of the tide gentle and pleasing.

Egros was really quite handsome, wasn't he? She smiled and took in the sharp cheekbones and straight nose. A nose that had never been broken. He looked young, but by his own admission, he was twice her age if not more. Something about paranormals aging slowly.

Yes, he sure looked tempting sitting in front of her, face a study in concern. He looked even better sprawled across the king-sized bed, naked beneath silk sheets, in the vision she was seeing as she continued to float on.

That long, lean body of his was like a swimmer's, with tight muscles and hidden strength. In her vision, Eg was wrapped around her, his pale skin the perfect foil to her golden brown. Those powerful legs and arms wound tightly around her gasping form. His long-fingered hands stroking, touching, caressing her everywhere while he whispered and grinned, and kissed her lips.

Dayum. Was that real? She wanted it to be.

Next, she saw them walking side by side through some woods. Could have been the forest that surrounded the Keep. Butterflies and dragonflies flitted around them, dancing in the breeze.

Egros was leaning down, saying something to her, and Margo, well, she was laughing gaily and carefree as she had never been before. The river in her mind grew wider, and scenes flitted by faster. Mostly of Egros and her, happy, then scared. Some men in dark suits were trying to take him away.

Mother appeared, and there was violence next, but she couldn't see what. Her heart squeezed in her chest, and panic filled her. She couldn't lose him. He meant too much to her.

Darkness came, and shadows seemed to overwhelm the scene. She couldn't reach him. Men in suits, Mother, and some faceless monster pointing with one gnarled hand. She felt his greed and lust, not for her but for Egros and something he had. This monster wanted to rip it from his body, his heart, his very soul.

She could not see him clearly, only felt his malice. And it was evil. Pure, unadulterated hate radiated from the monster like toxic sewage from a chemical plant. She could not let him get his decrepit fingers on Eg. Not while she was still breathing.

No. NO!

"No!" she yelled aloud.

"Margo? Margo? Come back to me, here. Are you okay?"

"NO! Wh-What?"

She blinked her eyes. She was panting, and sweat was dripping down her face. She was still there, trapped somewhere between shadow and fear. But slowly, she came back to herself, and her focus was on him.

Egros was crouching in front of her, both hands on her face. She couldn't recall details of what she had seen, but her pulse was still racing. Her heart was pounding. Confusion filled her, but it was quickly replaced by relief.

She shoved away the doubt and social constraints that would have prohibited such a thing, and the next thing she knew, Margo vaulted into his arms.

"Thank God," she whispered, holding him tight to her chest.

"Easy, I got you," he whispered.

His arms came around her like steel bands, holding her tight to his lean, muscular body. In that moment, the only thing she wanted to feel was the profound joy that had swelled inside her like the tide the second she saw Eg and registered he was alive and well. Not in the clutches of some faceless madman, but living, breathing, and with her.

Thank fuck, he was with her.

Margo was not used to feeling such strong emotions. As a marine, a lawyer, and a DPCA agent, she'd learned to compartmentalize her feelings. How else could she live and see the things she'd seen? But this wasn't the same. This was emotion so raw and powerful, it knocked her off her feet.

"Are you okay? Margo?" Egros repeated himself.

"Not really," she said, leaning back.

"But I am going to be," she said and slammed her mouth to his.

For a second, she thought he was pushing her away, but Egros was only standing up. His hard lips firmly sealed to hers. Those long arms she was starting to really believe she loved, like loved *loved,* tightened around her in an unbreakable embrace as he held her close. *So very close.*

Egros nuzzled her face with his, prodding her gently until she tilted her head the way he wanted her to. Then he growled against her mouth, and it was all kinds of sexy. Margo leaned into him, breathing him in as his tongue pressed inside her mouth.

She sighed, opening for him, allowing him to explore her mouth. Nothing had ever felt so right. Her hands reached up and wound around his neck. He was so tall, she had to stand on tiptoe, but she did not care. The deliciousness of it all was way too sweet for silly worries like that. She hadn't had enough deliciousness in her life, and Margo sure as fuck was not about to squander it away with worries.

It had been a long time since she'd been kissed stupid by a man, *er*, Witch, or anyone really. And Margo really liked to kiss. She wished she'd had a mint, or maybe practiced more or something in her youth. Anything to keep him there, kissing her.

Embarrassing? Maybe. She just didn't want Egros to ever stop. Of course, that was when he leaned back, eyes blazing red and chest heaving from being breathless.

"What? Is it bad?" she asked, concerned.

"What? No, hell no," he replied.

"Good," she returned, leaning up to kiss him again. But the damned man leaned back farther, and he was just too tall for her.

"It's just, um, are you sure about this?"

"What?"

"This here. You, me, kissing, touching, *um*, maybe, *er---*"

"Are you trying to ask me if I am sure about sex?"

"Yes. That. Very much that," he ground out, and pink stained his cheeks.

Fuck, he was adorable. Was she sure about sex? Yes. Margo was surprised to discover she was, in fact, very, *very* sure.

"Margo," he whimpered when her tongue snaked out to tangle with his. "I don't want to take advantage---"

As if any man could ever take advantage of her. The Witch had a few things to learn about Margo Wells, but she could teach him later. *Much later.*

Like when they were sweaty and spent and starving from exertion, when the high of being alive and being with him eased. Though Margo was pretty sure he would always evoke such feelings.

It was crazy. It was fast. And proof or no proof, she was pretty fucking sure it was magic.

Yes, her heart and brain both screamed aloud. Being with Egros was pure magic. And she reveled in it.

"Egros?" she said, breathing him in.

"What?" His voice was deep and gravelly with need, sending spirals of desire shooting through her already amped up body.

"Shut up and kiss me."

Chapter Twelve

He'd never been one for public displays of affection, not that is office was public but still. Egros was more a bedroom, lights off, locked door, kinda Witch.

Passion had never overridden his senses before. Certainly not like this. Then this saucy little vixen spoke, and he was helpless to do anything but obey.

"Shut up and kiss me."

How could Egros refuse a command like that? Especially when it came from the one woman in the world he wanted more than any other. Hands down.

His cock ached, heart squeezed, and magic pulsed all in time with his desire for her. Hell, he would've given her anything she wanted, anything at all for a single kiss.

He tried to control himself, told himself this was Logan's sister and he best not act too rash. Then she asked him for more in that husky voice of hers, and all reason went out the window.

Egros was hers to do with as she pleased. If she wanted kissing, then fuck yes, he would kiss her. Damn fucking straight, he would.

Egros would have kissed her for hours and been content. Only the feisty little vixen had other plans. Margo already had her hands down his pants, and whatever brain cells he had left jumped ship.

Egros hissed out a breath as her fingers closed around his cock. Fuck, that felt amazing. She squeezed and moaned while doing so, as if she enjoyed touching as much as he liked being touched.

Fucking hell.

He went cross-eyed at the sharp sting of pleasure from her caresses, the vixen using her nails against his skin, adding a bite to the sweet sensations and making his blood hotter than Hell itself. Having been to the Underworld, he could vouch for the temperature.

Of course, Egros' dick had been rigid since the moment he'd laid eyes on her. In truth, he'd been walking around fighting a semi boner for the last four days. But there was no fighting it now.

Not when she was wrapped around him like a python, and her delicious mouth was sealed to his. Margo pushed against him, and ass that he was, he let her go.

Well, of course he should let her go! Fuck's sake.

He wasn't an animal. He wasn't even a Shifter. Egros was a Witch. They didn't have fated mates and animal urges, but right then the Fates themselves sure as fuck could've fooled him.

His magic was pressing against him, demanding he take the woman and bind her to him. In fact, he almost thought he heard the word *mine* ringing clearly in his ears.

What the actual fuck?

Egros shook it off, allowing her to step back. He'd been raised a gentleman, and gentlemen stopped when a woman said stop. It might feel like it was going to kill him, but nothing an ice cold shower and some mind-numbing work couldn't cure.

Don't be so sure of that, his inner asshole snarked.

He closed his eyes, telling himself to shut the fuck up. The little bit of brain power he had left was currently busy reminding him to breathe, so he was a little deaf when she'd opened her lips to speak once more.

"I'm sorry, what did you say?" he asked.

Margo grinned, and that smile damn near knocked him to his knees. How was it legal for one woman to be so damn beautiful? And sexy to boot! And how could she be so calm when he was fighting the urge to bend her over the chair and take her hard and fast---

Fuck.

He really needed to stop thinking like that or he was going to embarrass himself.

Truth was, there wasn't enough cold water in the reservoir that piped into the Keep's many bathrooms to staunch his need.

Double fuck.

He was going to need an ocean to put out the fires of lust burning inside. Maybe two. Desire raged like a blazing inferno, and he couldn't recall ever feeling quite like that.

"Tell me you have a condom," Margo repeated.

He stared. Wait. What? She licked his lips, kissing him and rubbing her sexy little body against his. The female was so soft and warm, her brown skin ravishing in the golden hued lamplight.

What the fuck? He was a terrible poet, and worse, he knew it. But she was perfect and worthy of more sweet words than a Witch like him was capable of.

Perfect. Mine, he thought.

"Eg? Condom? Where?" Margo asked again, biting on his lower lip.

The sting of pain sent zips of pleasure right to his aching cock, and Egros growled and pulled her tight against him. Kissing her neck, he bit the flesh there, loving the moan that escaped her lips. He was still unclear what brought this on, but he was not going to question it. He couldn't.

"Condom. Now. Now. NOW!" she said, slapping at his arms.

"Top drawer," Egros growled.

Ever since Elena had mated Logan, the couple had been responsible for piles of condoms all over the damned place. Annoying at first, but he was grateful now.

He sucked on her tongue and tugged on her lower lip with his teeth. So sexy, so hot, she wiggled and writhed, making him mindless with every ministration. But no, that wasn't true. His mind was right there, every step of the way.

What was he doing making out with Logan's sister? Reason tried to push its way in between the passion exploding between them, but his magic pushed back, zapping him right in the ass so that he moaned once more into her mouth.

She kissed him harder. Her hands winding through his hair, and all his objections faded away under her sensual assault. Egros was putty in her hands. Well, not really.

He was more like rod of steel in her hands, but he wasn't about to repeat that aloud. Made him sound like a 70s porn star.

Fuck.

She smelled so good, like sunshine and daffodils. Good and clean and sweet. He wanted to treasure her, to keep this kiss sacred in his mind forever. Without him really conscious of it, his magic rushed forward, taking a snapshot of that kiss, and sealing the memory of it in 4D for him to keep always in the palace inside his mind.

"Mmm," she moaned, as if she too had felt and approved of the gesture.

She kissed him deeper, her breasts pressed against him so tightly he felt the unsteady beating of her heart against his skin. And that was when Egros Pyke said goodbye to his own heart.

Willingly he let it go, sending it to her as only a Witch could, in a sacred spell whispered only in his mind. He would love his sweet Margo until the end of time with every inch of his being.

She had the most incredible mouth. Plump lips

soft as pillows, sweeter than cherries, and did he mention demanding? Gods, he loved the way she got rough and demanding with him. Not afraid to show him what she wanted at all.

Margo placed two hands on his chest and pushed. She shoved him backwards, till he landed softly on the small sofa in his office. Before he had a chance to ask her again if this was what she wanted, to second guess what they were doing, she was back. And good lord, the woman got down on her knees in front of him.

Egros swallowed, eyes wide as he looked into her lust filled eyes. He knew this had nothing to do with the potions and spells he'd tried to erase her memories. Something had happened to her, something magical.

He felt something inside her he couldn't quite explain. She seemed hellbent on hiding it, but whatever it was, Egros had sensed magic. And it was coming from her.

His attempts at wiping her memories had not worked. But something had occurred. Whatever this attraction between them, he needed to know she was acting with free will. Then, as if she had read his mind, she spoke.

"I am very in control of myself, Egros Pyke.

Something happened back there, but before we talk about it, I need you inside me. I need to be close to you. To feel you. I'll beg later if you want me too, but right now, I need you to take these off," she growled and tugged at his pants almost as rough as a Shifter would have.

"I don't need you to beg, love. I just need to know it is me you want."

"You, only you," she whispered, caressing his face.

He didn't think twice again. Egros snapped his fingers and his clothes disappeared. Hers too.

"Oh fuck, that is so hot," she whispered.

One soft hand reached down and stroked his dick, the other gripped his knee to keep her steady. Then the little minx leaned forward and licked him from balls to tip, closing those sexy fucking lips of hers over the head of his cock.

Egros moaned aloud, back arching as she sucked him deep into her throat. His pulse raced, heartbeat roaring in his ears. Her scent surrounded him, filled him, and his magic pulsed and sizzled in response. Fuck, if she didn't stop, he was going to come.

"Stop. Won't come without you," he growled, and she sat back, grinning like the Cheshire cat.

Margo rolled the condom down until it covered

his cock, then she straddled his thighs. He leaned forward, sucking one taut nipple into his mouth. She tasted even better than she looked. Her gorgeous curves and all that golden brown skin, so smooth and hot, like warm silk, he thought as he slid his fingers along her firm thighs.

Egros could not get enough of her. She was fire and light, elegance, and grit, and he was completely in thrall of her. Margo lifted herself high, positioning him at her entrance.

Her eyes sparkled all gold and green as she lowered herself ever so slowly. Egros held his breath, watching every nuance of emotion flicker across her gorgeous face as she took him deep inside her tight pussy.

"Oh!" they groaned in unison.

This was beyond his scope of expertise. He was a Witch, not a gigolo. But damn him if he could not admit this was the most incredible, the hottest, the best damn sex of his whole life. If he ever said differently, Egros would be a fucking liar. And he was not that. Other things, maybe, but never that.

"You done?"

"Huh?" he asked, unsure of what she meant.

"You done thinking?"

"Uh, yeah."

"Good. Cause when you fuck me, I need you to be here with me. Only me," she commanded.

"Yes, of course. I am here with you, Margo. Only you," he growled, sucking on her neck.

"As long as we understand each other," she said, then rocked her hips.

Egros growled, knowing full well the minx had the upper hand. He nuzzled her skin until he found her plump nipple again. Pulling it into his mouth, he sucked hard, and was gratified when her pussy squeezed him tighter.

A pull and tug on the other nipple, and Margo was moaning aloud. Egros grinned, pressing her breasts together with his hands, he flicked his tongue from one bud to the other, back, and forth, harder faster, and she rewarded him for his efforts by fucking him harder and faster. He took the right nipple between his teeth and tugged, causing her pussy to tighten around him.

Egros growled with the bud inside his mouth, then he tugged again. Margo was whimpering as she rode his cock, faster and harder. Every time his teeth tightened on her bud, the little minx's pussy spasmed.

One more tug had her coming hard and hot all over him, her sheath squeezed him with every ripple and jerk of her orgasm, body tightened like a whip-cord until she slumped against him, breathing heavy.

That was when Egros turned her, so she was facing the armrest of the sofa. He pressed down on her back gently, and she went, lowering her face and arms so she was gripping the fabric between her nails. Margo was breathing more easily, but not for long. Not if he had anything to say about it.

By the time he was finished, he wanted her gasping for air and calling his name. Fuck, yes. He ran his hands down her back, cupping her ass cheeks and spreading them. He circled her back entrance with his thumb, loving her gasping moans as she pushed her perfect peach of an ass back into him.

Fuck, what a sight!

He took his cock in his hand and rubbed it against her pussy, still using his thumb to play with her ass. Margo whimpered and moaned, wiggling to try and get him to push deeper. He gave her an inch, then another, pulling back when she got greedy, only to give her more when she stayed still. Finally, she growled at him, and fuck if that wasn't sexy as all hell.

"Dammit, Eg," she said.

"Tell me what you want. You just have to tell

me," he whispered, his voice so low he barely understood himself.

"I want you inside me. Fucking me. Not-oooh---oh fuck, yes!"

Egros didn't wait for her to finish. He plunged deep inside, ramming into her hard and swiftly. She had him so riled up, he couldn't think, he could only feel.

So, he did. Egros felt. Her. All of her.

Fucking her relentlessly, he felt his magic roaring through him. The power he'd kept locked away pulsing in the pendant at his throat. Fuck, he needed to keep control, but then Margo was moving her sweet ass against him, and he couldn't concentrate on anything but her.

Her back bowed as she begged him to work her harder. How could he do anything but? Egros let go of the leash he had on his emotions, then he really started to plow into her. His hands held her hips so tightly he was bound to leave bruises, but fuck, it felt so good. And from the sounds she was making and the response he was getting from her body, she loved it.

"Yes, yes. Oh god, Eg!" she yelled her nickname for him, and surprise surprise, the moniker was already growing on Egros.

Their lovemaking was fast and furious, and fuck it all, amazing. Egros wanted the female to be his, longed to mark her somehow, someway. But Witches didn't do that. Did they? Fuck if he knew.

Egros didn't know much of anything right then. He didn't want to know. Only wanted more of Margo. Fuck, he wanted all of her. And so he took, and took, and in taking, taking, *taking*, he gave, gave, *gave* everything he had.

Egros offered her everything. All of himself. His hopes, dreams, wishes, and more. Everything that made him Egros Pyke, Guardian of Chaos and Witch. He poured it all into the sweet, sexy little vixen who bucked and bowed beneath his ministrations.

And when they came, they came together. It was long, and poignant, and glorious. Egros felt a wave of pure, white hot pleasure rush through him as he clutched at her hips and breasts with his hands. The rush was both sweet and surreal. It went on and on and on.

When they were both sweaty and spent, nothing more than a tangle of loose limbs draped across the couch like lifeless bolts of fabric, he admitted the cold hard truth even if only to himself.

Egros Pyke was in love.

Chapter Thirteen

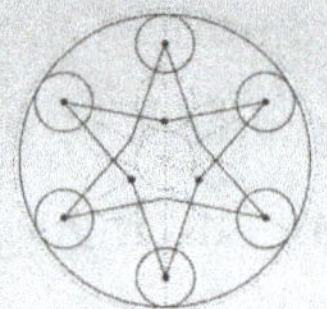

Margo woke up alone and deliciously sated. She stretched and stood, trying to make sense of what had occurred.

She'd agreed to let the Witch brainwash her, or whatever. But the potions he gave her didn't work on her messed up brain. Instead, she'd found herself floating along a river of absolute consciousness. That was where her memories were stored and visions of future events yet to pass swam.

The future was never certain. She'd read enough fantasy books to accept that. But something had happened there. Something real and beautiful, and if she wasn't careful, she would lose herself too it.

Her clothes were in a neat pile at the foot of the sofa. They appeared cleaned and folded. By magic, she guessed with a rueful grin. The Witch never did admit to anything, but he sure as fuck made their clothes disappear like lightning when she'd come onto him with lascivious intent.

She dressed quickly, since there was no shower in the potions room or whatever the heck they called it. Her stomach rumbled, and a snack sounded very good right about then.

Margo had no sooner walked into the room than every Shifter in the immediate area turned their glowing eyes on her. She froze, feeling like a piece of meat at a carnivore convention, fingers itching for her gun. But that wasn't the end of it. Oh no, Elena, Furio, Fergie, and Storm all tilted their heads towards her, and *sniffed*.

Freaky shit.

"What's going on?" Logan asked, taking a bite of the perfect red apple in his hand.

"Uh, nothing. Got anymore of those?" she asked.

"Basket," he said, munching on his piece of fruit while jotting notes.

Elena was elbowing him in the rib, and her fathead brother still didn't look up. Margo rolled her eyes and grabbed an apple, then scrounged around the cabinets for some peanut butter.

"My goodness, stop elbowing the poor man

when he's working. You know he can't hear you, right?"

"Logan," Elena hissed, but he just nodded and tilted his head to kiss her.

The Panther accepted the peck he gave her but growled something about idiot men. Not that Margo could blame her. Logan did turn into an inattentive idiot when he was on the verge of solving a problem.

"Elena, you got a question to ask me or something?"

She decided to put the woman out of her misery. And clearly, the others too, since they all moved forward, surrounding the kitchen island where she sat down with her snack.

"So, Margo, why do you smell like my man Egros?" Furio asked, right before his mate stomped on his foot.

"Really?"

"Ow, Jess! What'd I say?"

Jessenia mumbled something, giggling, when the big guy wrapped his arms around her. He nuzzled her neck and said something that caused the shorter woman to blush prettily.

All of the Shifters seemed to constantly touch their significant others. A hand on the arm, a kiss on the cheek, fingers toying with their hair. But none of it was aggressive or proprietary. It all seemed gentle and loving to Margo, and she was an excellent judge of these things.

"Um, Margo," Jessenia began, to Margo's utter amusement.

"Yes," she replied, slicing her apple into perfect slices before smearing the right amount of peanut butter on each one.

"We were wondering, though it is really none of our business, but um, why do you, um," the woman hedged.

Her cheeks were turning a delightful shade of pink, so Margo thought it prudent to draw this painful process out as long as humanly, *or inhumanly*, possible. Discomfort, other people's, not her own, was one of Margo's favorite things.

"Look," Furio butted in, clearly the impatient one of the gang. "We just wanna know why you smell like Egros."

"Is that what you want to know?" Margo asked.

"Yeah."

"I see," she replied, taking her time to bite and chew. "Any particular reason you all want to know this?"

"Egros is one of us," Storm inserted himself into

the conversation. "We care about him, so if you are using him- OW!"

"Geez! You guys have all the subtlety of a couple of army tanks in a church!" Fergie growled.

"Really, get out, all of you, or I swear you are not eating tonight," Jessenia said.

The men all grumbled, except for *fathead*. Margo's genius brother was still plucking away in his notebook. Clueless. Yes, the man was totally clueless, but he was her brother and she loved him.

"Okay," a very pregnant Fergie said, rounding on her.

"Two questions. First one, are you going to finish that?" she asked, pointing at Margo's half eaten plate.

"I was planning on it, but I am a good sharer," Margo said, offering the now drooling female a bite of peanut butter smeared apple.

"Thank you," she replied, munching on the treat and moaning happily.

"Second question, is Egros any good in bed?"

Margo's mouth twitched. The man himself was standing in the doorway, eyebrows raised at Fergie's impertinent questions. He stood silently, waiting for her reply with one eyebrow arched perfectly over curiously gold eyes.

She was going to have to ask him about his

revolving change of eye color, among other things. Her chest seemed to warm with his nearness, and she was surprised to find she felt aroused as well. What was she doing in the kitchen with these females instead of in bed with her man?

Her man. Where the heck had that come from? She was not sure, but she liked it. There was definitely an affinity for that kind of possessive terminology in the most basic part of her brain.

"To answer your questions, Fergie, first, you can have the rest of my apple. And second, I don't know, we never made it to the bed."

Then Margo stood and moved across the room. An uncontrollable need to kiss him burned inside her, overwhelming reason and decorum. She grabbed him by the collar of his black shirt and pulled him down for a kiss.

The sounds of gasps, whispers, someone clucking their tongue, and a whistle reached her ears, but Margo didn't care. Let them watch. All she wanted was to kiss the man, the Witch, standing in front of her. The incredibly sexy Witch who was kissing her back like he was starving for her.

"What the hell are you doing to my sister?"

Ugh. The fathead was still there. Before she

could tell him to back off, Logan had stormed over and tried to pull them apart.

And that was when Margo learned Magic was real. Because the second her brother had laid his hand on her, her sexy, hot as fuck Witch boyfriend, zapped Margo's twin with a bolt of magic so powerful, he went flying across the room in a cloud of purple smoke.

"Holy shit!"

"Logan! Are you okay?"

"What the fuck, Egros!"

"Hey, that wasn't me!"

The cacophony of voices rose to a deafening roar until, well, someone actually roared. That someone being a grumpy ass Dragon holding a squalling, red faced newborn in his massive arms.

"Does someone want to explain what the f-word is going on here?"

"Um---"

"Well, the thing is-"

"You see..."

"Quiet!" Margo yelled, turning to face the angry Dragon.

"I think I just zapped my brother."

Everyone went silent at Margo's declaration, which was good because she wasn't finished. Her pulse was racing like mad, and she felt dizzy. Somehow, some way, she'd sent her brother hurtling across the room like a shot without laying a single finger on him.

"You?" Elena asked, bending over Logan's prone form.

"Is he okay?" Margo returned.

"I mean, he's unconscious, but yeah, he's not bleeding or broken," Elena said, though she could tell the female was pissed.

"Good," Margo said, turning to face Egros who was frowning and looking at her curiously.

"Are you alright?"

"No. Um, put your arms around me," she said.

Thankfully, Egros did just that. His swimmer's build was deceptively lean, but she knew he was more powerful than other guys who boasted gym built muscles.

His strength was to the marrow, and it was just one of the many things she liked about the Witch. Unsurprisingly, she liked a whole lot about Egros Pyke. What she knew, anyway. And she planned on learning more.

"Margo?"

"Excuse me, everyone," she said, and passed out for the first time since she'd drunk way too much

Black Sambuca at a party when she was in law school.

She never drank the hard stuff anymore. All because of that one fateful night. Being underaged hadn't stopped her, but puking her guts out for days on end afterwards sure had.

Didn't matter now. Whatever Margo had done to Logan, it had used up a lot of her strength. Having Egros catch her before she fell to the floor seemed like the best way to go in her humble opinion. He looked down at her, cradled in his arms, eyes purple with worry before hers closed.

She'd wanted to tell him it was okay, but the truth was Margo wasn't sure if it was okay. Sleep was pulling her under, and she couldn't fight it. Not now. So, she gave in.

With any luck, she'd dream of Egros. The gorgeous Witch was already filling her dreams, she thought. Before her mind went blissfully blank, two words flashed across her sleepy brain. She wasn't sure what to make of them, but Margo would worry about that when she woke.

Egros.

Mine.

Chapter Fourteen

"**I** told you to take her memories of this place, Egros. What the hell happened?"

Kingston's grumble was lower than normal in deference to the now sleeping child in his arms. Holley was getting some much needed rest, and the Alpha Dragon was on daddy duty.

Egros sort of knew how he felt, seeing as how he'd been unable to let go of Margo ever since she'd asked him to hold her. More like told him, really.

"Can't you put her down yet?" Logan said unhappily from his chair.

Elena was holding an ice pack on his head where it had collided with the bottom corner cabinet. Egros felt bad about it. Well, not really. He would have, if the man hadn't been griping at him for the past hour and a half.

Egros gritted his teeth against the snarl that rose in his throat at the man's question. Witches did not snarl, for fuck's sake.

"No. For the eleventh time," he said in his most reasonable voice. "I cannot put her down. There is something going on here that we need to examine more closely---"

"Why don't you start by telling the story about how you magicked my sister into fucking you, you bastard? Tell us that one, so I can rip your goddamn head off!" Logan retorted.

"I think you are forgetting who you're talking to," Egros answered, his magic building inside him at the man's insolence.

It rose and rose until he felt it surround him, covering him and Margo in gold and amber circles of magic. It was odd. He'd never manifested magic this way, but then again, he wasn't certain it was even his.

"Everyone calm down," Kingston commanded, and the weight of his Alpha voice was felt by all in the room.

"Fine, but he needs to know Margo is an adult. She makes her own choices. And she chose to be with me, Logan, whether you like it or not."

"I don't like it."

"And I am really not interested in your opinion."

"That is still no reason to use magic against him, Egros," Kingston said, and Egros could tell he was disappointed.

Now for the hard part, he thought.

"Yes, Kingston, about that. You see, it wasn't me who zapped him."

"What do you mean?"

"Yeah, right," Logan muttered.

"He wouldn't lie. Not ever, and certainly not about this," Elena said, surprising even Egros by taking his side.

He glanced down and saw Margo looking up at him, her eyes dreamy with sleep and glowing faintly of purple and gold. She blinked and the glow was gone, replaced by her usual hazel green color.

"He means, it was me," she said, reaching up to touch his face with her warm hand.

Egros turned his head slightly to kiss her palm, loving the way her eyes flashed at the gesture.

"Are you alright?"

"Are you always going to ask me that?"

"Yes."

"I thought so," she said, smiling and using his arms to balance herself as she sat up slowly.

"Ms. Wells, how do you feel?" Kingston asked.

"Fine, but Eg's right. I zapped *fathead* when he tried to pull us apart. I don't know how I did it. But it was definitely me."

"Then he did something to her when he fu---"

Several growls sounded, but none as loud as Margo's own distinct cluck of displeasure.

"Logan Wells, you may be my brother, but I fuck who I want to fuck. And I do not ask you for permission, are we clear? Or maybe you need another zap," she said.

"No. Sorry. I was just worried, Gogo."

"Fine but keep a civil tongue in your mouth please and thank you before I get Auntie Beth after your sorry ass."

Egros knew she was bluffing, but damn, if he didn't enjoy it. Margo slid off his lap and sat next to him, but she kept her hand tightly clasped in his. A gesture he liked way too much to be healthy.

"Eg is just telling you what he knows, and it isn't any more than I do. He did as you asked. Gave me vials to drink, but it didn't work like he expected."

"She's right. If Margo were any other normal, she'd be back in her own life right now and we wouldn't even be a memory to her," Egros explained.

"What are you saying? My sister is a Shifter?"

"No, not a Shifter," Egros said. "I believe your sister is a Witch."

After an hour of Margo going over the events as she'd experienced them, with Egros chiming in with his own perceptions, they left Kingston alone to do some digging. It was after dinner, and Egros' stomach was growling. It stood to reason she was hungry as well.

"Want to get some dinner?" he asked impulsively.

"Yes," she replied easily.

"Italian or Chinese?"

"How about Indian?"

"Wonderful. I know a place that does an extraordinary biryani."

"Great, just let me use the restroom and I will be right with you."

"I'll be waiting," he said.

Smiling as he watched her walk down the hall to the room she'd been using, Egros ran a hand over his head. Fuck, this was moving fast, but he couldn't help it. Everything was easy when he was with Margo.

Nothing else seemed to matter when he was with her. Not his clothes, or his name, or his magic. She just put him at ease if there was such a thing.

He liked her. Loved her even, though fuck knew it was too soon for that. He wanted her, that much he knew. Everything felt right when she was with him, and his magic went wild whenever she was near.

Yes, it was rash to ask her to go out, but he really wanted her to go with him.

Someone knocked on Margo's door just as she exited the bathroom. She really needed to wash her face after that crazy power nap.

Her phone hadn't gone off in days, but she dropped it in her pocket, anyway. Force of habit, she figured.

"Who is it?" she asked, but that was all she got out before a slew of women filled her room.

Fergie, the pregnant redhead, was munching on a bag of chips. She was followed by Jessenia, also pregnant but not eating, Elena, and a tawny skinned woman with long, straight hair holding a baby.

"Hi, I'm Holley," she said softly. "So Egros really asked you out to dinner?"

"How do you all know that?" Margo asked.

"Shifters. We got good ears," Elena winked.

"Okayyy," Margo replied. "So, I am going to dinner with the man. What do you want?"

"Um, well, we just wanted to help," Holley returned, but Margo just stared blankly.

"Fine, you need it plain and simple, right? Well, the thing is, we all love Egros, but he is a stick in the mud. But he seems to like you, and we want to make sure he has a good time."

"Are you trying to get me to have sex with him? You know we did that already---"

"OMG! TMI!" Elena growled, covering her ears, and closing her eyes like a six year old forced to eat lima beans.

"Look, you just can't go dressed like that," Jessenia explained, rubbing her tummy.

"Okay, I am pretty sure if we just think about it a door should pop up here," Holley said touching the wall.

Margo was about to tell her she was nuts when suddenly, a large wooden door appeared where nothing, but wall had been moments earlier.

"Yup, here it is. Welcome to *The Ladies' Room*," she said, grinning.

Inside, Margo was stunned to see rack after rack of beautiful gowns and designer clothes. It was as if these women had their own personal department store right inside the Keep. Even better were the shoes and boots, all things she'd liked in fashion magazines over the years. Most were beyond even her budget, and amazingly enough, they were in her size.

"What is this place?"

"The Keep is filled with many spirits, and they like us to be happy," Holley explained, cooing at the now awake baby in her arms.

"He is beautiful," Margo said.

"Thank you. He will be strong like his father, but smart like me," she replied, eyes twinkling.

Margo smiled and, with Holley's permission, touched the baby's perfect little head. He was truly beautiful and seeing him secure in his mother's loving arms sent pangs of longing through the badass lawyer turned government agent.

Odd. Very odd.

"Okay, so with your hair and eye color, I am seeing greens and golds. Oooh! How about this?"

Fergie waddled over to a rack of clothes overflowing with exactly the kind of designer clothes Margo had always admired but shied away from. Flowy wide-leg pants that rode low on her hips and crop tops were not exactly the right fit for her job.

The DPCA did not have a policy on it per se, but

she'd always gone with fitted slacks and button-down shirts. Simple, plain, professional. Plus, she could carry a weapon under her many blazers without it showing. Not that she used her gun very often.

"That is beautiful," she said, ruffling the fabric between her fingertips.

"And perfect for dinner. Come on, take that off," Fergie replied, snapping her fingers impatiently.

"Fergie! Margo, ignore the pregnant psycho. You can use the divider to get changed and only if you want to," Jessenia emphasized.

Margo took the bundle and snorted at the women's antics. They must be really good friends, she thought, and a part of her longed for that kind of camaraderie. She'd never made friends easy. The curse of being the only child of an extramarital affair. Logan was her friend, but he was her brother so he kind of had no choice.

She dressed without even realizing it, pondering her sudden melancholy. She was being silly, Margo decided, stepping out from behind the divider. Holley was standing between Jessenia and Fergie, who were involved in some sort of pregnant lady slap fight, and Elena was looking through a rack of tall skinny jeans that only she could wear out of the four of them.

It all seemed so friendly. Comfortable, warm, and crazy. Like a family, she guessed. Everyone stopped whatever they were doing when she cleared her throat, and Fergie was the first to speak. Margo was really starting to like the nutty redhead.

"Damn, Egros is gonna shit when he sees you!"

"Um, I know I am still learning the vernacular, but is that what we want him to do?" Holley asked.

"She means, he's going to love it," Jessenia interpreted.

"Oh, I see."

But the confusion on Holley's face was evident even as she nodded. Margo grinned, and Jessenia rolled her eyes at Fergie. Baby Greyson cooed, and Holley's attention was diverted, but Margo couldn't fault her. The baby was just perfect.

"You look really good," Elena said, and the woman looked pensively. "Egros is a good man. Despite what happened."

"Logan told me about it," Margo confessed.

She'd known since day one about his trying to stop her brother and the Panther Shifter from getting together. She'd been mildly interested, but after recent events, Margo had to admit, she was downright curious.

"We never, um, you know," Elena said, pink eyes

going wide with what Margo assumed was embarrassment.

"I know that too," Margo said, and somehow, she simply did.

"He was just trying to help. And our kind, you know, *supernaturals*, don't trust easily. Anyway, I didn't want you to get the wrong impression. I've partnered with Egros in the field and couldn't ask for anyone better to watch my back. He's proven his loyalty time and again."

"Thanks, Elena," Margo said. "I appreciate it."

"I just, well, don't hurt him, Margo. That's all, I guess."

Elena rubbed the back of her neck, clearly uncomfortable with the discussion, but Margo stepped forward and took her hand.

"I get it, Elena. And I could say the same thing to you about my brother. Logan is all I have in the world."

"I couldn't hurt him if I tried," she replied easily, and the love she had for him shone in her bright pink eyes.

Amazing, Margo thought. The power she felt in Elena's grip, and the love shining in her eyes, told her the woman was complicated and powerful, and even better, she truly loved Margo's brother. That was good.

Something was changing inside of her. Margo felt as if something deep within her had been asleep her entire life, only awakening now in these walls and with these people.

Elena seemed confused by their conversation, but Margo got the message. Even if the woman did not understand, she did.

These people loved Egros. He was their family. And as she turned to the mirror and saw herself, curly hair down around her shoulders, pale sage crop top and wide linen pants with slits up the sides revealing her legs with every step she took in the leather sandals on her feet, she was stunned.

For the first time in memory, Margo looked relaxed and happy. Her brown skin was practically glowing, her smile radiant, and her hazel eyes were more green than gold at the moment.

"Dayum, I look good," she announced, and the other women stopped their chatter.

"You'll do," Holley said, nodding.

"Hell, with any luck Egros will be *doing you* before dessert!" Fergie replied crudely.

Margo just laughed and covered her mouth with her hand, stemming the snort that threatened to escape. These ladies! They were hilarious. And she couldn't have asked for a better group of women to be around.

"Margo?" Egros' voice drifted in through the walls, and she turned with bright eyes to see the door gone.

"Where is he?" she asked the women.

"Oh, the guys aren't allowed in here. This is our space. Just walk up to the wall and the door will appear," Holley explained.

"Magic," Margo whispered.

And it was.

Chapter Fifteen

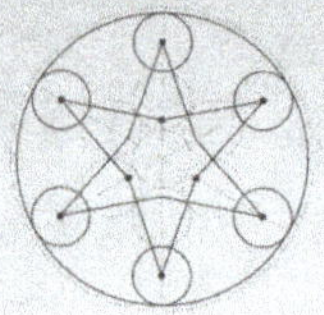

Egros started to wonder what the heck was going on after twenty minutes had passed agonizingly slow, and still no Margo.

He walked into her room, anxious when he saw it empty. Using his other senses, he quickly found a magical residue in the air. It was familiar, good. The *manetuwak*, he realized. The spirits of the Keep not only worked hard to keep the Guardians and their mates safe from outside forces, but they also used their powers to see to it that most every need was met.

Which included *The Ladies' Room*, a place for the females of the household to gather, chitchat, and try on Fergie's ridiculously large collection of designer shoes. Egros wondered how his Margo would fare with those four women. He wasn't worried.

His vixen could hold her own with anyone. Hell, he'd never seen a more competent woman in all his life. He waited another ten minutes, but patience was not his strong suit. Without any other recourse, he simply called her name.

Then she appeared. Like magic. Well, she used a door, actually. But *that* had appeared like magic.

"Holy fuck," he murmured.

Having only ever seen her in black slacks and button-down shirts, the change was surprising. Hell, he could hardly keep his tongue in his mouth. She smiled at him, as if she knew exactly what he was thinking. Soft linen, so thin it was sheer in places in sages and golds hung from her rounded hips in flowing waves.

With long slits up the sides of each pant revealing her gorgeous curvy legs with each step, and a crop top in the same material leaving her midriff bare, she was a vision. Like a goddess from Ancient Egypt, or maybe one of the Greek Pantheon.

Margo's smile was mysterious and intoxication, Mona Lisa, but better. The woman was gliding towards him, nothing as mundane as walking for his sweet vixen.

For fuck's sake.

His cock was fighting a losing battle with his pants. The blasted thing threatening to bust a hole through the fabric, he was so hard. Egros' heart was pounding as she neared him, the woman was so damn beautiful she stole his breath. Margo stopped just short of touching him, and he thought he'd die from lack of contact.

"Ready?" she asked in a husky little whisper that had him closing his eyes and gritting his teeth.

Fuck yes, he was ready, for anything, everything. For her. Only her.

Mine, his magic growled.

"You said Indian food, right?" she asked, bringing him abruptly back to the present.

"Yes, if you like."

"Sure," she replied, shrugging.

She raised her eyebrows, and he damn near tripped over himself leading the way. Egros stopped short, then turned and took her hand.

"Please, after you," he said, remembering himself.

"You don't have to treat me like a prom date, Eg."

She laughed, and he loved the sound. He was acting silly, but he couldn't help it. He wanted this date to be perfect, and he hadn't been on many. Come to think of it, he hadn't been on any.

Sex, of course, but that had been an equal exchange based on need. Egros had never had a real relationship with a woman, except for the women at the Keep, and those were all purely platonic.

"Is the restaurant far?" she asked, stepping beside him.

"Far? Well, I suppose."

"How long till we get there?"

"Oh, we will be there in a few minutes."

"How if it's far?" she asked, cocking her head to the side, and sending a mass of curls tumbling to her shoulder.

Fuck, she was beautiful. So much so that he didn't really understand her question. He just took her hands, placing them on his chest. Then he moved his to her waist.

"Hold on," he whispered near her temple.

Egros closed his eyes, casting a simple transportation spell that he'd used a million times or more. A magical wind rose around them, and Margo gasped in delight. She shuddered against him, but he held her safe and secure. He would never allow harm to befall her. Not ever.

The fact she trusted him meant the world to

Egros. He vowed then and there to endeavor to keep her trust for as long as he lived. She might not know it, but he wanted more than a date and a night with the beautiful woman. Much more.

"The best place for biryani," he said, once the wind had died down.

"Oh, my god!" Margo gasped, clasping a hand to her chest as she looked around at the busy Kolkata street.

The air was warm and full of spices since they were in a market district with restaurants and shops aplenty. Evening was falling and tourists and locals milled about, some exploring, others going on with their daily business.

"We're in India?" she whispered, and Egros smiled.

How could he help it? He nodded and took her hand, so they didn't get separated in the crowd.

"How did you do that?"

"A spell," he replied, easily.

"Magic. You used magic? I thought you weren't going to show me any of that," she replied.

Her eyes were bright with excitement, and he felt ten feet tall, knowing she was impressed. A small hint of worry and doubt snuck inside his brain as they entered a local establishment and found a cozy table for two.

It was a fact that Margo had been looking for proof of magic her entire life. Now that he'd shown her some, what if that was all she wanted? What if she planned to reveal him to her superiors at the DPCA?

All the doubts of his youth came creeping in while perusing the menus, and Egros' spirits fell. What if he had read this wrong? What if she was just looking for another round of what had transpired earlier between them before outing him and his fellow Guardians to some normal government agency?

His cock was willing, but his heart almost beat right out of his chest. Pain at even the thought of her doing such a thing filled him. Fuck, how was he supposed to find the truth?

No, his magic seemed to shout at him. Looking at Margo as she navigated the menu, asking him questions while sipping the steaming tea a waiter had brought for them, he knew she was enjoying herself.

"I can't make up my mind. Can we just get one of everything?" she laughed.

"If you like," he replied easily.

"I know! You pick. I trust you," she said.

And those words washed away every doubt that threatened to crumble his happiness. Egros lifted their still joined hands and pressed his lips to her palm, love for her filling him.

She was amazing. An honest, good, and fierce woman, beautiful as she was brave, and he was proud to be with her.

"Everyone is staring," she whispered, her hazel eyes glowing with emotion.

"Americans always get looks when visiting foreign places," he explained.

Though Egros was used to that kind of thing, he had a feeling they were staring because she was just so gorgeous. He'd been to this part of India before, and it should have been old hat, but not now. Not with her. With her everything was new.

They ate and laughed, shared stories about their lives and antics. He loved her enthusiasm, her joy. She was as real a person as he'd ever known. He was in love for the first time in his life, and the real truth, was Egros was terrified. He was a powerful Witch, but he had no idea how to not fuck this up.

"Furio really did that? I mean, he totally looks like this Jersey wise guy type, but really? He picked up the guy and threw him in the river?"

"Well, he wasn't really a guy. He was a marine Shifter, and he was being a total ass."

"I see. And that makes it better?"

"No, not really, I guess," Egros replied, laughing with her.

"Ice cream for dessert?"

"I love ice cream."

"Good, come with me."

Egros paid the bill, and they walked hand in hand to the alley where they'd arrived. He didn't see the men tailing him until it was almost too late. But somehow, Margo had. Her hand tightened in his, and before the first spell hit them, she'd turned around and raised her hand.

Purple and gold light emanating from her palm, and Egros was so stunned he could not move. Wait, that wasn't why he was suddenly frozen. Something was pulling on him, on his magic, and his knees buckled.

"Egros! What do I do?" she yelled over the loud din of magic blasting through the air.

But he could not answer. His voice was stuck in his throat. It was like his strength was being siphoned and he could only watch in horror as a tall, black cloaked stranger faced off against them. The others were still trying to zap them with weaker spells, but Margo's deflection spell was holding.

"Give me what's mine, boy!" snarled a familiar voice, and Egros' eyes went wide.

"Eg, who is that revolting piece of shit?" Margo asked, her eyes glowing gold as the man Egros had not seen since he was thirteen years old pulled off his hood.

Time had not been kind to Bartholomew Pyke. His face was wrinkled and ravaged with pockmarks and scars that had not been there when Egros had last seen him. He looked wild and manic, like a junky who'd gone too long without a fix and would do anything trying to score.

"Need you to let go," he finally managed.

Margo, quick as she was, looked down and dropped his hand. She pulled a small caliber gun from a thigh holster he hadn't even known she was wearing and aimed it at the two goons now siding with his father.

They were Witches but had obviously been messing with Dark magic. The deep scars and missing appendages, fingers, noses, and more, he could only imagine, told Egros they'd been practicing blood rituals to commune with Demons. A sort of power bartering system that rarely worked out for the Witch involved.

"The magic! It is mine!" Bartholomew raged, but Egros did not waste time on him.

He wrapped an arm around Margo's waist and transported them out of there. Once they were safe and back in his room at the Keep, he ran his hands over her, checking for injury.

"Are you hurt? Were you hit?"

"I'm okay. Hey, Eg, I'm okay," she said, taking his face in her hands. "Tell me what's going on. Who was that man? Were they Witches? I felt magic, but it seemed wrong," she said, brow furrowing in confusion.

Egros sat down heavily on the bed. He ran his hands over his head and face. How to explain the sordid details of his childhood? Hell, his very existence.

"That man was Bartholomew Pyke," he confessed. "He's my father."

Chapter Sixteen

"*He's my father.*"

That was probably the last thing Margo would have expected Egros to say after their run in with some magic spewing thugs. She sat down beside him and waited. Her years as a lawyer, and an agent, had taught her silence was the best tool to use when someone wanted to confess something. And Egros clearly had something to say.

"My mother was a young, innocent Witch from a powerful line. When she'd met my father, she'd been visiting relatives in the area. He was the head of the Pyke Coven and looking for a way to replenish the magical stores he, and those in his family before him, had squandered."

"Magical stores?"

"Yes," he said, and she could feel his anger, though it was not directed at her.

"You see, Margo, magic is finite. There is only so much of it in the universe. It can be passed down from generation to generation or willed to another. If you are a less scrupulous Witch, it can be bartered, bought, and sold.," he explained hurriedly.

"I see."

"No, you don't. Not yet. But I will continue to explain, because you need to understand that with magic there must be balance. If used inappropriately, there is always a cost. It is not the stuff of fairytales and animated movies. You can't just squander it without consequence."

Egros heaved a sigh, and she felt his worry and grief as if it were her own. Not knowing what else to do, she moved closer, allowing her leg and hips to touch his. Confident she was on the right track when he didn't shy away, she stayed there, waiting.

"My father killed my mother. I have no real proof, but he did. He wanted her magic, but she'd already willed it to me. Her family had ancient powers, huge stores of magic that would be dangerous in the wrong hands," he said, voice so low it was barely above a whisper.

"Then she did well, leaving it to you," Margo said, her belief ringing true with her words.

"I don't know," he replied sadly. "I've never even unlocked it. You see here, this stone pendant is the key to my inheritance."

He lifted the necklace he always seemed to wear, and she studied it. The stone seemed to simply float inside a silver circle, hanging there by magic, she mused. Why she hadn't noticed that before, she could not say? It was beautiful, hauntingly so. Sadness filled her at the thought he'd never tried to unlock his mother's gift to him. That he'd never felt worthy of it.

"I thought my father was dead, you see. So, I figured I had time before I tried to unlock it, to see what was there. Besides, my mother told me the time to reveal the power within would choose me."

"Wow. You were never curious?"

"Sure, I was, but Margo, the thing about magic is it's seductive. Like any kind of power. Did you notice the missing fingers and scars on my father and his men?"

"Yes."

She'd been taken aback by the horrendous appearance of the three men with long black cloaks who'd followed them into the alley. Margo had been on the best date of her life, and she figured they were going to try to mug them. Imagine her surprise when it turned out to be some sort of attempted magical robbery instead.

"Dark magic requires sacrifice. It is the most forbidden craft, and yet, it is used by those desperate enough to try and barter with Demons for power."

"Demons exist too?"

"Oh yes, my sweet innocent. There is much in this world and the next that you don't know. And you are better off not knowing. I'm sorry. I will try to find some stronger spell so you can forget---"

"What? What are you saying?"

"This was a mistake. All of it. You shouldn't be here---"

Margo flinched and moved away from him. He might as well have slapped her! It sure as fuck would have hurt less. Her heart squeezed so hard she couldn't breathe. How was it possible for him to walk away? To even think it!

"I'm not made of glass, Eg. And we already proved I can't be brainwashed or whatever the fuck you call it," she snapped.

Her chest heaved with the effort it took to breathe, and Margo stood up, pacing back and forth in his room. The jerk! She was angry at him for even suggesting she was too weak to stand beside him.

"Am I magic?"

"What?" he asked, truly stunned.

"Am. I. Magic."

"Uh, well, you have used magic. I can't be sure, not exactly. But tonight I felt as if you were pulling it from me."

"So, what am I?"

"Margo, I don't have the answers you are looking for---"

His eyes were a sad, deep blue as he looked up at her, but she would not be swayed from her line of questioning. She was on to something here, even if he was in denial.

"I can't be just human. I have had visions of the future, glimpses, my entire life. When I first saw you after I busted through that window, I felt like I knew you, Eg. And when we kissed, it was like coming home."

"Margo," he growled, and the sexy sound sent a wave of arousal washing over her.

"I know you are upset, and that is understandable. If I was facing the man, I believed killed my mother, I'd be pissed as hell too. But don't push me away to try to protect me, Eg. I am stronger than I look."

"Fuck. I know you're strong," he growled, and stalked her to the farthest wall.

"Do you know that? What else?" she asked, desperate to know.

This Witch had her so wrapped up in feeling, she didn't know whether she was coming or going. Wetness coated her sex, her pussy throbbing with need as he neared her. She'd never been turned on so fast in her life. Everything was different with Egros. It was better, hotter, more honest, and even fun.

Life was not perfect, and neither was she, but it was magical. He was magical, and she wanted to be with him. She couldn't imagine being without him. So yeah, when he'd even suggested she leave, she'd gotten angry.

Margo never got angry with anyone except Logan. And that was because her fathead brother worried the shit out of her. If she lost him, she'd be all alone. In fact, Margo had never had anyone to call her own. Except maybe now she did.

Was Egros hers?

She swallowed audibly.

Holy shit.

Another swallow, followed by some deep breathing.

I love him.

The realization stunned Margo. She might have thought it earlier, but now it wasn't just an idea. It was fact. She didn't just love to fuck him. She loved *loved* him.

"Do you think I am weak, Eg? Is that why you're pushing me away?"

She watched emotions play across Egros' face. His eyes shifted from blue to teal to gold to that deep purple she loved so much. They stayed that hue when he'd made his decision, anticipation made her tremble.

"Weak? Fuck, no. You are not weak. You're strong, and gorgeous, and fucking mine. You hear me, Margo? You. Are. Mine. Mate. Conpar, Mine," he growled.

He smelled so good. Rosemary, mint and sex, pure unadulterated sex. Need rose like the tide, and she couldn't help herself. Margo grabbed him by the collar and tugged him down to meet her hungry lips.

She was so done with talking. Pure satisfaction had stroked her, like hands, when he made his declaration. It was primal and possessive, and she fucking loved every syllable. She wanted to be his. Need to be. Just as she needed him to be hers.

"Mine," he growled between kisses, and she felt something pulsing between them.

White hot and delicious, it danced across her skin, and his, engulfing them both in purple flames. Magic, she thought with wonder as he stripped off their clothes with a wave of his hand.

Egros' hot, hard body held hers against the wall. He lifted her with minimal effort, and she wrapped her legs around his waist, moaning as he entered her swiftly and without error. Margo was so wet, soaked for him, allowing his long, thick girth to stretch and fill her in smooth stroke after stroke.

His tongue plunged into her mouth in time with his cock, and she could only hold on and enjoy the ride. Fuck, it was so good. He was so good. Fucking her against the wall, hard and fast, his magic covering them and touching them everywhere.

The sounds of their flesh slapping together filled the room with their grunts and pants a close second. Margo's pussy clamped around him, holding tight as the first wave of ecstasy swept through her. Egros growled, his kisses traveling from her mouth to her throat. He licked her neck, teeth grazing her skin while his cock pounded into her aching cleft.

Fuck, so good. So close.

The magic surrounding them burned brighter, hotter, going from purple to gold to white as she started to come. The pendant around his neck started to smoke, and as he pumped once, twice, three last times, spilling his seed into her, the thing broke.

"Margo!" he roared her name, cock still pulsing as he came, and came, and she came right along with him.

Her orgasm crested, and Margo's mouth opened in a soundless scream. Never had she felt such intense pleasure. So good, it bordered on pain. Then it was pain. Actually, owie fucking pain.

"Fuck, oh fuck, oh fuck!" she screamed, and Egros released her slowly, lowering her to her feet.

"What's wrong?"

"Eg?" she gasped in question as the broken pieces of the pendant lifted off the floor. "Are you doing that?"

"No! I'm not. Margo?" he yelled.

But it was too late. The stone was whipping around her until the silver circle rose, level with Margo's heart. Then both stopped, joining once more, stone inside the circle, and both struck, slamming into her chest and sending white and gold lights into the atmosphere, practically blinding them both.

The force of that thrust propelled her back into the stone wall, but Egros was faster. He'd moved like lightning, fast as any Werewolf she'd ever tracked, to cushion her body before she could make impact.

She'd have told him she appreciated his gesture, but it was wasted since her chest was burning hotter than if she'd been shot. Margo grunted against the pain, and just when she thought she couldn't stand it, it was over.

Whatever force had been holding her upright, it ended with that final punch of pain that had so suddenly stopped. Margo slumped down. She was conscious, but not physically. She would've hit the ground had Egros not caught her.

"Margo? Are you okay?"

"Eg?" she asked, staring at him in wonder.

Fear and worry tainted the air with an acidic smell that made her nose twitch, but it was Eg's strange appearance that had her wide eyed.

"What is it, love?"

She sat up slowly, hands touching his face. His now very hairy face. He covered her hands with his, stopping when he felt the beard now coating his cheeks.

"Let's get you up," he mumbled, standing and lifting her easily.

"What happened?" she asked when he dropped her gently on the bed.

Egros did not answer as he sat beside her and summoned a mirror in front of them. She was always awed when he used magic, but it was getting easier for them both, she mused.

Margo was rubbing the spot on her chest that still burned a little when he scooted behind her. His face was back to normal, no more hair. But as for Margo, well, she was not one hundred percent herself.

"What the heck is that?" she gasped, looking at the mirror, then down at her chest.

"I think that is my mother's pendant, love."

"But it is in my chest!"

"Yes. Now, don't freak out. I am sure there is a good reason---"

"Egros, did you do this?"

"No, I swear it. Tell me, when you saw me before, when I was worried for you, was it just a beard that suddenly grew?"

Margo turned her head to look at him. She liked his big warm body around her. Loved what they had just done to one another, even though it ended rather strangely. But how was he so calm?

"What? Your beard? Who cares about a beard? Wait a sec," she said, closing her eyes to bring back the memory of only minutes before.

When she'd been concentrating on her own pain, Egros had somehow changed. Her best guess was that his fear had spiked some sort of magical adrenaline rush, except his reaction was bizarre, to say the least.

During her years with the DPCA, Margo had watched and gathered intelligence on various Wolf Packs and Bear Clans, and the one thing those Shifters had in common was they were fiercely protective of their families. Their husbands and wives in particular, though they used the term *mates*.

When Egros thought she was hurt, he'd responded the same. He'd started growling, and once that happened, his body began to morph. Purple and gold flames engulfed him, transforming him from the Eg she knew and loved to something else. Something bigger, badder, hairier. He was like some sort of bipedal Wolfman.

"Here, I have an idea," she said and lifted her hands to his head. She couldn't articulate what she'd seen, but maybe she could show him.

Once she started concentrating, it was like a whole new world opened to Margo. A world within his mind. She gasped at the pleasure, knowing she was sharing information, sending it directly into his head.

And it wasn't just visions she sent him, but her feelings, and something else, too. Something wild and pulsating, powerful and slightly willful, she discovered when she tried to coax it aside.

Magic. It was magic. And it was theirs, she felt the truth of that and Egros' ready acceptance instantaneously. Emotion filled her heart, and Margo felt tears slide down her cheeks.

"I can feel you inside my head, love. The magic, it's so great, so much of it, and it belongs to us both. Can you feel that?" Egros spoke in whispered wonder.

"Is it hurting you?" she asked.

"Not at all. It is amazing, love. You are amazing!"

"So, what does it mean? What happened to you? And to me," she said letting go and turning back to stare at the stone and silver circle now embedded in her skin.

It no longer hurt, and she frowned as she touched it. Strange that it was not raised, either. It felt like her skin, like it was a sort of magical tattoo.

"My mother told me love was the key to her magic, but I assumed she meant her love. I was wrong," Egros said. "She meant you, and my love for you. I think we are soulmates, Margo Wells. And I know I love you more than anything else in the world."

She closed her eyes at his words. Was it true? She'd never had much affection in her life, but she wanted it. Here and now. Margo wanted Egros' love and affection. And she wanted to give him hers in return.

She turned around and straddled his legs, felt his hard cock slide between her slick folds. She wanted him so badly, but first she had something she needed to say.

"I love you too," she told him, lifting up to take him in.

Eyes on each other, they made love with nothing between them. No lies or pretense, no secrets, or hidden expectations.

Only love. And this, Margo thought, this was the real magic.

"I love you, my *conpar*," Egros growled, the new animalistic side of him coming out to play as their passions rose.

"I love you too," she replied, moaning in earnest as he lifted his hips to meet her downward thrusts.

Faster and harder, Margo rode him, loving the way his new powers had him growing fur and fangs with his increased desire. The rumbling growl in his chest as he suckled her breast had moisture dripping down her thighs, and when her orgasm hovered out of reach, her sexy Witch licked the surrounding skin of new tattoo and that was all she needed to start coming.

And so on it went, all through the night, Margo and Egros loved on each other, insatiable for one another. They shared their bodies, minds, hearts, souls, and magic with one another, filling the void that had kept them so lonely for so long.

"It was worth it," he murmured before drifting into sleep.

"What was?" she whispered.

"A lifetime alone to finally find you. I love you, Margo," he said, and she sighed, snuggling closer.

"Love you too."

Chapter Seventeen

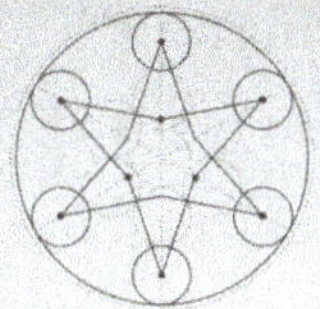

"You did what?"

"I, um, *magic bonded* with your sister," Egros told Logan the next day over breakfast.

"What the fuck does that mean?" he snapped.

Egros scratched his head, he was far too happy to let Logan's annoyance bother him. He'd hoped to catch everyone at breakfast, and he was lucky enough to do just that.

Holley was off nursing Greyson, but everyone else was there. It was confession time.

"I sent a question to the Morrigan a few days ago when I started noticing things about Margo and myself," he began, eyes flashing to where his conpar was sitting, looking at him sweetly.

She was cunning, his mate, and he was so damn in love, she was all he could see. Dangerous for some, but for him, like with other Guardians, it meant being the best version of himself. One who could better protect her and magic at all costs.

"You sent a request to Sherry Morgan-McAllister without consulting me?" Kingston asked.

"Forgive me, Kingston, but this was a Witch matter and there was no other recourse."

"I see," the Dragon replied and gestured for him to continue.

"I had always operated under the assumption that Witches do not have mates, and that something was wrong with me because of my, well, oddities even as a child. Turns out I was wrong and right."

"How do you mean?" Jessenia asked.

"I've always felt hollow, alone," he said, turning when Margo joined him.

"Me too. I love you fathead, but you know I never had many friends or family who loved me back. Just you and Auntie."

"Oh, Gogo, why didn't you say anything?"

"Cause, I had books and school and my jobs to keep me busy. I didn't need you worrying about me," Margo said.

"Now that I have found Margo, and she's found

me, things are different. I felt a pull to her the second I saw her, and now I know why. You see, way back in my mother's lineage, the Morrigan has discovered an ancient line of Druids, *shape shifting* Druids."

"Is that like even a thing?" Fergie asked.

"Yep," Margo replied, grinning.

"It is," Egros added. "I have a fated mate. May I introduce you all to Margo Wells, my conpar."

His mate giggled and leaned into him, and Egros readily wrapped his arms around her, nuzzling her neck with his nose and lips. Daffodils and sunshine, mixed with a hint of his own rosemary mint scent.

Perfection.

The table erupted with questions and congratulations, but he only had eyes for his sweet, feisty, and *so fucking beautiful it hurt* Margo.

"What about her job? I mean, doesn't she like want to out us and everything?" Furio asked.

"Actually, I think it is time Kingston and I have a chat about the DPCA. I think we can work together, maybe share information, and sort of stay out of each other's way. After all, you guys could use someone on the inside to help with covering things up, can't you?"

Egros knew she'd piqued Kingston's interest when the Dragon raised one eyebrow. He grinned and let go of her hand when she moved to sit down next to the Alpha.

"Margo is special, you know," Logan said from beside him.

"I know."

"Good. So, then I don't have to tell you that if you hurt her, I will develop an elixir to strip the skin off your ass while you sleep, right?"

"Um, no, Logan, you do not have to tell me anything like that."

"Logan," Elena said, rolling her eyes. "He's just kidding. Sort of. Okay fine, not really," she growled when her mate just stared at her.

"But, like I already told him, if she's your mate, you would never hurt her."

"Of course, I won't I love her, Elena."

"Good."

"Um, who are those guys?" Fergie asked, pointing her oatmeal laden spoon towards the large window.

"Fucking hell," Egros growled when he recognized the same two Witches who had attacked him and Margo in the alley the day before.

Another second and his father entered the clearing in front of the Keep. The bloody bastard!

"I've come for what's mine," Bartholomew Pyke

sneered. "Are you still the sniveling brat I left behind? Too afraid to face me," shouted the old man.

Long ago, Egros would have been scared. But not today. Not when he had so much to protect.

"Who the fuck is that guy? And what happened to his ear?" Storm said, moving in front of his pregnant mate.

"That is my father. And I will deal with him."

"Not alone, you won't," Margo said from beside him.

Egros looked down. He hadn't even seen her move, but there she was, eyes blazing. Every instinct inside him was screaming at him to order her to stay put, but he could not do that. Margo was a warrior in her own right. She wouldn't appreciate him stifling her. He just had to make sure nothing happened to her, or else he'd burn the whole fucking world down.

"We can't have that, can we?" she asked, looking into his eyes as if she'd read his mind.

Holy fuck. She had. Egros' eyebrows disappeared into his hairline, but she just grinned and nodded.

"I love you too. Now, let's go kick your dad's ass."

"Sounds like a plan," Kingston said, joining them.

"I can't ask you to do that. This is my fight---"

"When is this cump gonna learn, we're family, Eg. Hey, I like that nickname. I think it's gonna stick."

Storm clapped a hand on Egros' back and for a moment, he felt like the kid he used to be when the big black Wolf used to come and watch over him.

"Fine," Egros said, overwhelmed with feeling. The fact the Guardians still accepted him after his past mistakes. That they would risk themselves for him was almost too much to bear.

"We're a family, Egros," Elena agreed.

"Um, the missing ear tells me he's made a blood sacrifice to some Demon. That means he is ripe with evil power. His minions, too. Be careful out here," Egros warned.

"You too," Margo replied, cocking her pistol and taking his hand.

Love thundered inside of him, and he'd never felt quite so strong. He looked at where his father was waiting, still shouting obscenities, and readied himself mentally to face the biggest monster of them all.

His father.

* * *

Margo noticed two things when she stepped into the courtyard beside her man, the other Guardians of Chaos flanking them. Jessenia, Fergie, Holley, and baby Greyson remained indoors, the spirits of the Keep would be protecting them as they watched worriedly at their mates and friends going off into battle.

First, Bartholomew Pyke was one ugly bastard, and Egros must have taken after his mother in the looks department. Thank fuck.

The second thing, he had more than two men with him. As they stood, half a dozen other Witches stepped out of the woods, hands ablaze with magic.

"I see you've grown more powerful. Good, more for me," Bartholomew spat.

"And you've grown simple, old man, if you think you will get even a drop of what is mine," Egros returned.

"How can a weakling like you ever hope to use your bitch mother's magic? It is mine, boy."

"Never weak, and never yours, father. Mother's magic is ours now. Go now, and live," Egros said, holding Margo's hand.

"You've given it to your whore? Ha! I will rip it

from her screaming body after I've killed you," Bartholomew said.

Egros growled and Margo seconded that emotion. The man who sired the love of her life was a foul, disgusting parody of a man. When she looked at him, Margo saw only darkness and evil. A creature totally void of all humanity.

That was the real difference, the link she'd been missing when studying the world of the paranormal. Magic was not just theirs. It belonged to everyone. The supernatural and the human. That was what the Guardians protected, and the realization made her love Eg even more.

Speaking of her man, Egros continued to growl as his father made threats against her. Her chest warmed and pulsed, and she felt power flow freely between them., covering the two of them with purple and gold flames.

Damn.

Her man was sexy when he was angry. His body began to bulk up slightly, and his power pulsed, mixing with hers. The Morrigan was looking into her heritage, but it did not matter what she found. Margo now accepted her visions as part of the magic that was always hers. Combined now with Egros' powers and that of his mothers, she was learning more about magic than she ever dreamed of.

Even better, she was learning what it meant to love and be loved. Really loved. And this pitiful excuse for a father was not taking that away from her. No way. No how.

The sounds of fighting grew, but she could not take her eyes off the scene unfolding before her. Margo watched as Bartholomew raised his hands and inky black tendrils of what she assumed was dark magic began to shoot out at Egros. Her mate growled as he deflected all but one, the tiny dark spiral escaped his spell and zapped a single curl right off Margo's head.

"Hell no," she growled. "Don't you know not to mess with a woman's hair?"

Egros threw his head back and roared, his form swiftly changing from Witch to the bipedal Druid Shapeshifter of his ancestors. They'd talked about what it meant to be a conpar, and she knew that Guardians were gifted with a special boon to their powers when they found and claimed their mates.

Last night, Egros had claimed her with his words, his body, and his magic. Margo, being a tough as nails modern woman, claimed him right back. She watched in awe as his body changed, increasing in size, strength, musculature, and hair, she couldn't forget that. His nails elongated into claws and fangs protruded from his mouth. Swirls of gold and purple magic surrounded him, and the same flames danced protectively along her skin.

Like a magic suit of armor, she thought. *Like a me sized shield.*

"What is this?" Bartholomew Pyke asked, fear tainting his voice as he looked at the beast that was his son.

"*This* is something you can't handle," Margo replied. "*This* is *mine.* And you really pissed him off."

Then it was her turn to stare as Egros charged his father. The Witches in his thrall came at her then, grabbing at her arms and legs while she sent magic shooting through her gun as she fired at them. Margo fell to the ground, more Witches came from the woods, hurling spells at her new friends.

They were weak, but many, and it took precious time to stop them. She tried to find Egros and saw him battling a large serpent made of black smoke that his father had conjured. The bastard was stronger than the rest, but she trusted Egros. Knew he would do anything and everything to make his way back to her.

The Guardians were holding their own, though Logan had been hit with a fireball that left him doubled over in pain. Elena's sleek Black Panther was tearing the throat out of the Witch who dared hurt her mate, and Margo nodded approvingly.

There were so many of them, she wasn't sure how to help. Then she closed her eyes as a vision came careening into her mind. It was fast and abrupt, but it showed her what to do. Margo turned to see a single puddle on the muddy and battle scarred lawn. She dropped to her knees and began to chant words that had somehow come into her brain.

A second later and the stagnant water began to swirl, deeper and wider it grew and grew, turning into what looked like a whirlpool that led straight to Hell's door. A sulfuric stench rose from the inky depths, and Margo stepped back.

"Toss them in here," she screamed above the wind, and Furio's Stallion turned, kicking one Witch right at the whirlpool.

Over and again, she worked with the Guardians to dispense of those Witches who had given their souls to evil Demons in exchange for drops of power. Every now and then, she could have sworn she saw a flash of fangs or glittering black eyes in the inky depths.

Beasts waiting for their feast, she mused and shivered.

She was no stranger to blood and gore. In fact, when it was her loved ones being threatened, she downright approved. As the battle died down, Margo found Egros with her eyes. He was standing over the prone body of his father. The man's remains turning to a black tar like substance before their very eyes.

His eyes met hers, the irises burning bright red. Her mate smiled then, love burning brightly in his gaze. Margo smiled back, sweaty and covered in mud and filth from the fight, but so in love and happy to find him unhurt that she wasn't paying attention.

That was when the Witch she'd thought she'd finished off grabbed her and pulled, tugging her down into the black pool that led straight to Hell.

To her death. To her end. Fuck.

"MARGOOOOOOOOOO!"

Epilogue

Egros ran towards where the bastard Witch had pulled his mate and despite the other Guardians screaming his name, he dove headfirst into the black pool. Straight to the pit. Straight to her.

"Margo!" he roared over the sounds of wailing and fire.

There were many levels in Hell, and not all of them were bad, to be honest. But this one was reserved for the damned. Souls, like his father's, who had bargained for more than they had to give.

He saw her then, being fought over by a pack of hellbeasts, unconscious and bruised. The Witch who'd dragged her there had already been gobbled up by the Demon he'd thought to ensnare. No others had come up yet, but they would. The smell of fresh meat too good to pass.

Fuck no, he snarled.

Egros' other form took over, the flames of his magic covering him and when he turned, he saw them surround her as well. One curious hellbeast got too close, and the magic zapped him, sending the creature howling. He raced to her side, snarling as others clawed and scratched at him, but he did not care for any injuries to his person. He only cared for her.

"Margo," he growled, his voice deep and gravelly as he scooped her into his arms.

Her clothes were bloody and torn, but he had her now. She was safe now. He turned his head, looking for the doorway out. The pool was starting to close, and he had to haul ass to get them there in time.

Time moved differently in Hell, so it wasn't surprising when he burst through to find snow on the ground and a plaque marking the spot where they'd gone under. Margo shivered, blinking up at him as he tried to catch his breath.

He was exhausted. Dirty. Starving. But so fucking happy to be back.

"Holy shit! It's them!" Storm shouted somewhere nearby.

The big Wolf tried to touch them, but Egros' magic wasn't quite ready for that. Purple and gold flames covered him and his mate. He watched her breathe, heard her sigh, and when she opened her eyes and smiled at him, he kissed her.

That kiss was worth a trip to Hell and back any day.

"*Egros!*"

"*Margo!*"

The other Guardians and their mates came running out of the Keep. Everyone had changed, he thought absently. Fergie was holding what he could only assume was her and Storm's baby, and happiness filled him in thinking the Wolf had a family of his own. Greyson was toddling beside his mother, and Kingston's eyes glowed brightly with feeling as he looked at where Egros was kneeling with Margo in his arms.

Jessenia's stomach was hugely rounded, and she must be due any day now, he thought, while Furio stood beside her, eyes wide. Byram was there too. The Vampire the only one who reached out with a cautious hand.

"Glad you're back, old fellow. It took you long enough," he grinned, revealing his needlelike fangs.

"Sorry about that," Egros said, still a little breath-less. "Hellbeasts were a bit of a problem."

"I see. Well, better get her inside then," the Vampire added.

Egros looked down to see snow was falling, and now landing on his mate. That wouldn't do. He stood and walked inside, nodding at his friends. He would explain it all later. Much later.

Egros used his magic to clean himself and Margo, she was still asleep, and he was too tired for an actual bath. Together, they lay down in bed and just slept.

On the third day of their prolonged slumber, Egros blinked to find Margo looking up at him, her hazel eyes wide and curious.

"What is it?" he asked, throat dry.

"You dove into Hell for me," she whispered

"Are you hurt? Shall I call Byram? He is the best healer we have---"

"Eg," she said, hands on either side of his face. "You. Jumped. Into. Hell. For. Me."

"I would do it again," he said, honestly.

"I know."

"I love you. My own. My mate. My conpar."

"I love you too, Egros Pyke. With everything I am, I love you," she said, and then she was kissing him, and everything else was forgotten.

His thirst and hunger, all of it flew out the window. Completely sated by his mate in his arms, where she belonged. Egros climbed up her body, determined to show her without words just how much he loved her.

He kissed every inch of her, sucked and licked, stamped himself on every inch of her glorious brown skin. Loving on Margo was better than anything. Her pleasure was his only goal, and filling her was the ultimate homecoming.

Hours later, they showered and dressed in loose, comfortable clothes. Then they went to the kitchen for some food. A feast waited on the table, and all their friends surrounded them.

"How did you know we would come out now?" Margo asked Holley, who was putting the finishing touches on a tomato salad with some heirloom varieties grown in her greenhouse.

"The *manetuwak* told me," she replied. "And since you are my sister Witch, I think it right I start teaching you what I know."

"I'm a Witch too?"

"Well, of course you are," Holley said, as if the question was ludicrous. "And he didn't need to bother the Morrigan with all that. She's here, by the way, over there."

Margo's eyes found his, and Egros smiled. It was what he'd always suspected, having confirmation was just icing. He turned to see a woman with mismatched eyes sitting down with Jessenia, her wild curly hair a myriad of colors as well.

"Come sit by me, Margo Wells. We have some things to discuss," Sherry Morgan said, calling his mate over.

Egros bowed at the female and nodded at Margo to go on. He knew his mate had so many questions about magic, and this was the perfect opportunity for her to learn. The Morrigan was the most powerful Witch alive, and he had nothing but respect for the female.

"Well Egros," Kingston approached him, and Egros averted his gaze in deference to the man's dominance, and out of respect.

"Alpha," Egros said, still looking down. Kingston waited a bit for the Witch to meet his gaze.

"I am so very glad you're back, son," the big Dragon said, embracing Egros in a tight short hug.

Shocked, but grateful, Egros nodded. He was too choked up to speak.

"Sorry it took so long. Time moves differently there," he explained.

"I understand. And you and Margo, both can tell

me and *Mother* after dinner," he said, nodding at a large, conspicuous man sitting at the table.

Egros recognized the name from when he was still interviewing Margo upon her arrival at the Keep. It seemed so very long ago. But that was a worry for another day.

Right then, he only wanted to eat and drink and simply be. The meal turned out to be fabulous, and as he laughed and made merry with Margo by his side, surrounded by friends and family, he came to one very real conclusion.

Life was precious, and it was good. Most of all, it was magic.

The Guardians of Chaos worked hard to keep magic free for all, but it was still a carefully guarded secret. The most important one in the entire universe. It was their job to protect magic and the chaos that breeds creation.

So, yes. Magic was a secret, but sometimes secrets were meant to be shared with one special person.

Margo was his special person. His mate. His conpar. She fulfilled him in ways he'd never thought he'd be lucky enough to experience. And that night, after they'd retired to their room and loved each other till they were breathless, he told her.

"Of course, I love you, I mean, who else would go all the way to Hell for me," she said, only half joking. "You risked your life for me, Eg. You shielded me from harm with your magic and your love. I don't know what I would do without you."

"You saved my life by loving me," he returned, meaning every word.

"And you will never have to find out what it's like to be without me, conpar."

"What are you saying?"

"I'm saying I want you to stay with me. Always. We are mated, but I know you were raised human, so. Marry me?"

"Marry you? Just like that," she asked, both eyebrows raised.

Nerves almost stopped his heart, then she smiled, and he knew his naughty little vixen was teasing him. Fuck, he loved this woman. From head to toe and everywhere in between.

"Yes, of course, I will marry you! I've been dreaming of you for years, Eg. You're my one. My only one."

"Thank the gods," he murmured, holding her naked body tight to his.

Margo raised her eyes to meet his and took his face in her soft hands.

"I love you, Eg. Always have."

"I love you too, so much more than I could ever have imagined."

And then he showed her.

Again, and again, and again.

T*he end...*

Did you enjoy this installment in the Guardians of Chaos series by C.D. Gorri?

Catch up with the rest of the Guardians today! Now available wide.

And don't forget to keep an eye out on more from this series and other Paranormal Romance & Urban Fantasy tales by subscribing to C.D. Gorri's Newsletter today.

Happy reading!

Vampire Shield: Guardians of Chaos 6

Book 6 in the Guardians of Chaos Series is coming soon!

He left her behind years ago. She's never forgotten.

The Loyalist Union of Logic and Order has a new leader, and they are threatening the balance of magic. Witches are being attacked, and Shifters kidnapped, their magic siphoned through ritualistic bloodletting, a dark and ancient Vampiric practice that had not been utilized in an age.

Byram Evers is the only Vampire with the Guardians of Chaos. His Alpha sends him to investigate the mystery behind the magic letting epidemic, and the trail leads Byram back to his former Clan.

And back to *her*.

Princess Kaelene of the Clan Withers has spent years obeying her father and bowing to the demands of the Vampire laws. Betrayed by love, she refuses all suitors, determined to live the remainder of her life alone. Then he comes back, and her world turns upside down.

Will Byram discover the truth behind the bloodletting and redeem himself to the only woman who ever mattered?

Click Here for Vampire Shield.

GUARDIANS OF CHAOS
VAMPIRE SHIELD
USA TODAY BESTSELLING AUTHOR
C.D. GORRI

Have you met my Bears?

Looking for a Paranormal Romance series that is loads of growly fun?

Meet the Barvale Clan first in the Bear Claw Tales!
A complete shifter romance series about 4 brothers
who discover and need to win their fated mates!

Followed by two more spin off series, the Barvale
Clan Tales and the Barvale Holiday Tales!

No cliffhangers. Steamy PNR fun. Go and read your
next happily ever after today!

Beware... Here Be Dragons!

The Falk Clan Tales began as my stories surrounding four dragon Brothers and how they find their one true mates, but when a long lost brother arrives on the scene, followed by a few more Shifters...what can I say? The more the merrier!

Each Dragon's chest is marked with his rose, the magical link to his heart and his magic. They each have a matching gemstone to go with it.

She's given up on love, but he's just begun.

In *The Dragon's Valentine* we meet the eldest Falk brother, Callius. He is on a mission to find a Castle and his one true mate, one he can trust with his diamond rose....

His heart is frozen; can she change his mind about love?

In *The Dragon's Christmas Gift* our attention shifts to Alexsander, the youngest brother of the four. He has resigned himself to a life alone, until he meets *her*.

Some wounds run deep, can a Dragon's heart be unbroken?

The Dragon's Heart is the story of Edric Falk who has vowed never to love again, but that changes when he meets his feisty mate, Joselyn Curacao.

She just wants a little fun, he's looking for a lifetime.

We finally meet Nikolai Falk and his sexy Shifter mate in *The Dragon's Secret*.

*Now available in a boxed set.

Look for The Dragon's Treasure in 2022!

Other Titles by C.D. Gorri

Other Titles by C.D. Gorri

Young Adult Urban Fantasy Books:

Wolf Moon: A Grazi Kelly Novel Book 1

Hunter Moon: A Grazi Kelly Novel Book 2

Rebel Moon: A Grazi Kelly Novel Book 3

Winter Moon: A Grazi Kelly Novel Book 4

Chasing The Moon: A Grazi Kelly Short 5

Blood Moon: A Grazi Kelly Novel 6

**Get all 6 books NOW AVAILABLE IN A BOXED SET:*

The Complete Grazi Kelly Novel Series

Casting Magic: The Angela Tanner Files 1

Keeping Magic: The Angela Tanner Files 2

G'Witches Magical Mysteries Series

Co-written with P. Mattern

G'Witches

G'Witches 2: The Hary Harbinger

<u>Paranormal Romance Books:</u>

<u>Macconwood Pack Novel Series:</u>

Charley's Christmas Wolf: A Macconwood Pack Novel 1

Cat's Howl: A Macconwood Pack Novel 2

Code Wolf: A Macconwood Pack Novel 3

The Witch and The Werewolf: A Macconwood Pack Novel 4

To Claim a Wolf: A Macconwood Pack Novel 5

Conall's Mate: A Macconwood Pack Novel 6

Her Solstice Wolf: A Macconwood Pack Novel 7

Also available in 2 boxed sets:

The Macconwood Pack Volume 1

The Macconwood Pack Volume 2

<u>Macconwood Pack Tales Series:</u>

Wolf Bride: The Story of Ailis and Eoghan A Macconwood Pack Tale 1

Summer Bite: A Macconwood Pack Tale 2

His Winter Mate: A Macconwood Pack Tale 3

Snow Angel: A Macconwood Pack Tale 4

Charley's Baby Surprise: A Macconwood Pack Tale 5

Home for the Howlidays: A Macconwood Pack Tale 6

A Silver Wedding: A Macconwood Pack Tale 7

Mine Furever: A Macconwood Pack Tale 8

A Furry Little Christmas: A Macconwood Pack Tale 9

Also available in two boxed sets:

The Macconwood Pack Tales Volume 1

Shifters Furever: The Macconwood Pack Tales Volume 2

The Falk Clan Tales:

The Dragon's Valentine: A Falk Clan Novel 1

The Dragon's Christmas Gift: A Falk Clan Novel 2

The Dragon's Heart: A Falk Clan Novel 3

The Dragon's Secret: A Falk Clan Novel 4

The Dragon's Treasure: A Falk Clan Novel 5

Dragon Mates: The Falk Clan Complete Series Boxed Set Books 1-4

The Bear Claw Tales:

Bearly Breathing: A Bear Claw Tale 1

Bearly There: A Bear Claw Tale 2

Bearly Tamed: A Bear Claw Tale 3

Bearly Mated: A Bear Claw Tale 4

Also available in a boxed set:

The Complete Bear Claw Tales (Books 1-4)

The Barvale Clan Tales:

Polar Opposites: The Barvale Clan Tales 1

Polar Outbreak: The Barvale Clan Tales 2

Polar Compound: A Barvale Clan Tale 3

Polar Curve: A Barvale Clan Tale 4

Barvale Holiday Tales:

A Bear For Christmas

Hers To Bear

Thank You Beary Much

Purely Paranormal Pleasures:

Marked by the Devil: Purely Paranormal Pleasures

Mated to the Dragon King: Purely Paranormal Pleasures

Claimed by the Demon: Purely Paranormal Pleasures

Christmas with a Devil, a Dragon King, & a Demon: Purely Paranormal Pleasures (short story)

Vampire Lover: Purely Paranormal Pleasures

Grizzly Lover: Purely Paranormal Pleasures

Elvish Lover: Purely Paranormal Pleasures

Hot Dire Wolf Nights: Purely Paranormal Pleasures

Christmas With Her Chupacabra: Purely Paranormal Pleasures

The Wardens of Terra:

Bound by Air: The Wardens of Terra Book 1

Star Kissed: A Wardens of Terra Short

Waterlocked: The Wardens of Terra Book 2

Moon Kissed: A Wardens of Terra Short

**Now in a boxed set and in audio!*

The Maverick Pride Tales:

SERIES MAKEOVER COMING SOON

Dire Wolf Mates:

SERIES MAKEOVER COMING SOON

Wyvern Protection Unit:

SERIES MAKEOVER COMING SOON

Standalones:

The Enforcer

Blood Song: A Sanguinem Council Book

EveL Worlds:

Chinchilla and the Devil: A FUCN'A Book

Sammi and the Jersey Bull: A FUCN'A Book

Mouse and the Ball: A FUCN'A Book

The Guardians of Chaos:

Wolf Shield: Guardians of Chaos Book 1

Dragon Shield: Guardians of Chaos Book 2

Stallion Shield: Guardians of Chaos Book 3

Panther Shield: Guardians of Chaos 4

Witch Shield: Guardians of Chaos 5

<u>*Howl's Romance*</u>

Mated to the Werewolf Next Door: A Howl's Romance

The Tiger King's Christmas Bride

Claiming His Virgin Mate: Howls Romance

<u>*Twice Mated Tales*</u>

Doubly Claimed

Doubly Bound

Doubly Tied

<u>*Hearts of Stone Series*</u>

Shifter Mountain: Hearts of Stone 1

Shifter City: Hearts of Stone 2

Shifter Village: Hearts of Stone 3

<u>*Accidentally Undead Series*</u>

Fangs For Nothin'

<u>*Moongate Island Tales*</u>

Moongate Island Mate

<u>*Mated in Hope Falls*</u>

Mated by Moonlight

<u>*Speed Dating with the Denizens of the Underworld*</u>

Ash: Speed Dating with the Denizens of Underworld

Hungry Fur Love

Hungry Like Her Wolf: Magic and Mayhem Universe

Shifters Unleashed Boxed Sets

Check out these amazing anthologies where you can find some of my books

and the works of other awesome authors!

Midnight Magic Anthology (Water Witch)

Island Stripe Pride

Tiger Claimed

NYC Shifter Tales

Cuff Linked

Coming Soon:

Werewolf Fever: A Macconwood Pack Novel 8

Arachne: Speed Dating with the Denizens of the Underworld

Sealed Fate

Air Witch (as seen in the Rituals & Runes Anthology)

Sweet As Candy (as seen in Once Upon An Ever After)

Spring Fling (co-written with P. Mattern)

For Fangs Sake

Tiger Denied

Moongate Island Captive

Hungry For Her Bear: Magic and Mayhem Universe

The Dragon's Surprise

The Dragon's Dream

Taming Magic: The Angela Tanner Files 3

Vampire Shield: Guardians of Chaos 6

Chickee and the Paparazzi: FUCN'A

Excerpt from Wolf Shield: Guardians of Chaos by C.D. Gorri

What a day! Fergie McAndrews headed towards the pick-up truck she'd borrowed from her roommate for work that morning.

Of course, the thirty-thousand dollar certified used luxury car she'd splurged on earlier in the year was in the shop. Again.

Just another in a long line of bad decisions. After leaving a perfectly good job for a startup company, she was laid off three weeks ago and had to borrow money from her parents to pay rent. Wasn't that humiliating?

"This is the last time, Ferg," her step-monster had said after she'd Venmo'd the money to her.

God forbid the mechanic call and tell her the car was ready. She wouldn't be able to pick it up for another week. That was when she got her first paycheck from her newest gig at L-Corp. Not a startup, but an older company with new offices in Bayonne, which was only a half-hour commute.

But to commute, you needed a car. Fergie had no choice but to borrow the old pick-up from her best friend and roommate, Jessenia Banks. It wasn't like she needed the truck. She worked from home these days. Besides, Fergie promised to fill it up and have it washed.

She huffed out a breath. It'd been a really long day. A crappy one too. Fergie wanted to love her new job. Really, she did. But so far, it was the pits. If Fergie wanted to be a librarian, she would've been one.

Research was her jam. Well, when it was interesting. She had a knack for sniffing out information and compiling easy-to-read spreadsheets and time-lines. It wasn't the hard work that annoyed her. Her complaint was the content. The actual stuff her new boss had her looking up. It was beyond boring.

Why an enormous conglomerate like L-Corp needed old land surveys, cross-referenced with newspaper reports on accidents, crimes, etcetera. She had no idea. She'd been at it for weeks now. So far, she'd researched six locations given via GPS coordinates across Hudson County. Her new boss wanted everything, every little insignificant piece of information she could dig up.

That was the easy part. It was the hassle of the actual job that really made her want to give up. Every day she had to drive to Bayonne to pick up her work laptop she'd dropped off the night before with all of that day's findings. Every single night they wiped her computer clean.

Like she was going to run away with the secrets of what happened on 2nd and Washington sixty-years ago. Can you say paranoid? Ugh.

Fergie had always looked forward to working for a huge global company. It was supposed to be her ticket out of the Garden State. Traveling the globe, seeing new things, visiting far-off places was always a secret dream of hers. Well, that, and having her own walk in closet full of gorgeous designer shoes.

Best secret dream evah! In her opinion, anyway. What woman didn't love shoes? Fergie hummed as she daydreamed about rows and rows of Blahnik's, Jimmy Choo's, Garavani's, Ferragamo's, and her personal favorites, Louboutin's on every shelf!

Don't judge. Fergie wasn't shallow, she just liked pretty things. Haters gonna hate. But every time she ran across a thrift or second-chance store, she'd search high and low to see what they had. That was how she'd scored the pumps on her feet.

They made her feel good about herself. Being five-foot two-inches short with more curves than a racetrack, Fergie had had more than her fair share of self-esteem issues growing up. Alright, so she was chubby. She could admit that proudly now.

If everyone looked the same, the world would be one boring as hell place. Fergie liked herself perfectly fine these days, in spite of all the times her step-monster tried to make her diet growing up. So she liked food and shoes. Big deal.

She worked hard to feed and clothe herself, so as far as she was concerned, no one had a right to comment. So what if she wanted some excitement in her life? Fergie was aware she was better off than most, but what was wrong with having goals?

She'd spent a lot of time thinking about how a woman like her could have an adventure. Travelling was the only thing she could think of. Of course, she'd been hoping this job would be the answer to that. Even travelling for work was better than being stuck.

Sigh.

So far, her plans had fallen flat, but hey, at least she was earning a paycheck. Her new boss, Mr.

Offner, might be a strange man, but he signed her checks, and that was enough for now. Fergie had never seen more than a glimpse of him. All of her instructions usually came via email.

Most of the time she was able to compile her research quickly, then she'd head back to the office to organize it into neat little spreadsheets, and finally, she'd hand it all in with her laptop. But not today.

Mr. Offner sent her an email detailing everything she could dig up on one of the oldest places on record in the county. Of course, land surveys that old, along with police reports, newspaper articles, deeds, and sales records were nowhere she could easily access them.

After wasting hours at both the court house and municipal building, Fergie had been directed to the *second* public library. Apparently anything over a hundred years old was filed away in the godforsaken place. She'd been shocked to find an entire room filled with musty old archives. And wouldn't you know it, there was no cell service and no internet access. Plus, their phone lines were down. She'd had to photograph each page using her cell. When she got home later, she would send those photos like a fax to her boss along with her spreadsheet. If she could manage that before collapsing into bed.

Excerpt from Bound by Air by C.D. Gorri

Troy Waman looked down at his smartphone to the little red arrow blinking on his map app, indicating he had reached his destination. He frowned pensively before shaking his head.

"What a fucking shithole," he murmured to himself as he exited the nondescript black SUV his Station Master, Rex, had given him for the job.

"Try not to scratch it," the tough Bear shifter had said with a barely contained growl after their meeting the day before last. After a thousand years of waiting, The *Wardens of Terra* were being called to duty and this was Troy's first assignment.

It took him a day and a half to make his way to Shadowland, New York from the little suburb in Virginia Beach where his Station was located. There were dozens of them across the continental United States and even more overseas, though he'd rarely been out of the county himself.

Troy rolled his shoulders and exhaled. He was the first from his Station to be called to duty. A fact that left him both proud and humbled at the same time. He'd trained damn hard since he was a child waiting for such an opportunity. Now he had it, and it was almost too much to bear.

Fuck and damn. It's time Troy, get your ass in gear. That was all the sympathy he had for himself. Why the hell should he have any at all? Troy Waman was no tenderfoot normal. He was a Warden of Terra. He didn't need to remind himself of the honor and duty that went along with his position.

The *Wardens of Terra* were an ancient group of elite warriors. All of them Shifters. Identified in their youth and trained throughout their preternaturally long lives, they were guardians as well as fighters. *Station Masters* led teams of Wardens across the planet.

Though they'd been deactivated sometime in the last millennium, Wardens were born, chosen, and trained every day with the distinct knowledge that someday, they'd be called upon to defend the earth. That day was here.

Troy Waman had been trained as a Warden since before he learned how to spell the word. His heritage was a mix of Anglo and Native American. His father's blood was a mix of tribes including Algonquin, Lenape, Cherokee, and a few others. He hadn't stuck around long enough for anyone to learn the rest.

He supposed he could get a DNA test, but that might raise too many questions with the normals. Especially in this day of advanced technology in biogenetics.

Besides, it was quite common in today's world to find Native American peoples descended from multiple tribes. Troy Waman was uncommon for an entirely different reason. He was a Shifter, a special race of dual natured beings with one foot in the supernatural world and one in the human. Troy was a *Thunderbird Shifter* to be exact. Something unique even amongst Shifters.

He stretched his long, lithe body as he stepped away from the vehicle. It was already dark out despite it being fairly early in the evening. *Daylight savings my ass.* He sniffed the frigid air. The unusually high winds made the cold seem even more bitter. The street lamp stuttered on the corner, a rusty fence squeaked, and a black cat crossed the street, ducking under some parked cars. Troy's frown deepened.

It looked like the setting of a B-horror flick. All it needed was some half naked co-ed to run down the street with a masked bogeyman stalking behind her, traditional blood-coated knife in hand. *Oh yeah.* They might call it *Shadowland Nightmare* or something equally cheesy.

He stopped his musings and used his heightened senses to take in the downtrodden area around him. It would seem upstate New York wasn't all orchards and sprawling suburbs. He smirked as the "I love New York" song ran through his head. *Yeah, right.*

Apparently, parts of the Empire State were as fucked up as the street where he was born in Newark, New Jersey. He'd visited that shithole back when he was in his teens just out of curiosity. What a mistake that had been! He'd left almost as soon as he'd arrived. His extended family had been, shall we say, less than welcoming.

His gray-haired grandmother had screamed and crossed herself when he stepped over her threshold. He was what they called a *skin walker*. They feared and loathed him as something evil. Him evil? Like he was the motherfucker who knocked-up some unsuspecting normal and left her ass with a Shifter baby.

He was not evil, but he was something they did not understand. He'd been angry and ashamed that day. He'd crashed through his grandmother's kitchen to hitch a ride back down to his Station in Virginia Beach.

In his youth it was more like a military training camp, but it was all he knew of home. After all, it was where he'd lived his entire life. He'd made his peace and settled fully into his life there.

The incident with his grandmother had happened over a decade ago, when Troy had stolen his records out of Rex's office. Still, the memory remained fresh in his mind as if it were only yesterday. The fucked-up street where he was standing only brought back the painful reminder that he'd come from the same kind of squalor. *Fuck this*, he thought.

The pungent scent of despair washed over him. *Reminding him.* A young man with a hood pulled up over his head, eyed him from the street corner. *Drug dealer. Shadowland* indeed. It was an apt name for this shamble of a neighborhood.

The young man continued to stare until Troy allowed his beast to shine through. His golden eyes pinned the errant youth through the inky darkness of the night. Startled, the kid dropped the bag he was holding and ran down the alley.

Punk. Troy walked over and picked up what he had so hastily left behind. A couple of grams of crack cocaine and heroin, *probably cut with Fentanyl.* There were also various sized baggies full of what smelled like some below average marijuana and half-rotted psychedelic mushrooms.

Just your garden variety of illegal substances to be found on most street corners in neighborhoods like this one. *Fucking normals.* He frowned and dumped the still sealed contents down the closest storm drain. He sent a quick text to Rex earmarking the location.

Rex would make sure the local police department got an anonymous tip to retrieve the narcotics before someone got hurt. Recreational drug use, mainly the opioid epidemic, was wreaking havoc amongst the humans with more and more of them succumbing to their addictions.

It was troubling, but not Troy's problem. Shifters were extraordinarily hard to kill. Most human drugs had little to no effect on supernatural beings. *Normals,* he growled the thought, *such weak creatures.*

To be fair, Shifters had vices too. He just had little experience with it. Cecil, a Station-mate of his, had an adrenaline addiction. He was always putting himself in dangerous situations, even during simple training exercises. Fernandez, a Jaguar Shifter, was always trying to get into some chick's pants. *Sex addict.* And he knew of others who channeled their energies into ways he considered to be mostly unproductive.

His opinion, for sure. He'd always been something of a loner by nature. There weren't many Thunderbird Shifters around. Hell, he was the only fucking one he knew of in this part of the world.

He didn't blame or judge his Station-mates for their proclivities. Most of the Shifters he knew had large appetites which included food, exercise, and sex.

Troy had certainly explored that part of him. He wasn't a man-whore or anything, but he'd had his share of women. None of them mattered to him. Just a means to satisfy the occasional itch.

Troy was determined to live his life as a Warden of Terra alone. He never expected to find anyone willing to share what was a potentially deadly existence.

Those who followed the Darkness and evil were

always looking for ways to gain the upper hand and it was his job to stop them. The way he saw it, it was an honor and a duty to serve.

He shared this great responsibility with the entire organization. The core belief of the Wardens was based on one indisputable fact Shifters had walked the earth since the dawn of time, even before humankind; therefore, they were responsible for the well-being of the entire planet and all its inhabitants. Especially those who were inherently weaker. Mainly females and *normals*.

There were other supernaturals who believed humans, or normals as they referred to them, were a blight on the planet. Those creatures wished to destroy them and take over.

Demons, Dark Witches, and a whole plethora of evil beings sought the destruction of the normals and the world they lived in. *Idiots! Did they even realize if they destroyed the world, there would be nothing left? Where the fuck would they live?*

Of course, the supernatural world had many agencies that worked towards the common goal of saving the planet. The *Order of the Guardians,* for example, were responsible for policing the various factions of supernaturals.

Shifters generally tended to ally themselves with

the Guardians. Sure, there were *bad* Shifters, but he'd never come across any willing to follow the Dark. Simply because most agreed the destruction of the world could not be allowed to happen.

Different Packs and Clans, etcetera, of course, had different ideas. Some wanted to remain secret, others wished to come out, and other still wanted to rule the weaker humans. It was a whole fucking thing, and they argued about regularly.

Troy didn't know from any of that. He spent little time in the human world. His efforts better spent making himself worthy of being a Warden. Training, exercise, and following orders. That's what Troy lived for, it was why he was chosen.

Thunderbird Shifters were very rare. *Special.* He scoffed at the stray thought. But no matter what way he looked at it, Troy was indeed unique. In more ways than one. He was born *marked* by the stars. A *Shifter of Terra.*

From infancy, he was told he carried the power of his sign within him. *Aquarius* ruled his destiny and it would aid him in the never-ending battle against the forces of darkness.

Every single Warden he knew was a Shifter like him. They were the fiercest warriors on the planet. Like many others throughout the last thousand years,

Troy, *a Shifter child who was marked*, was taken from his parents and trained by his Station Master until the time when he would be called into use.

All that time, he thought, *and here I am*. He tried to ignore the pressure building inside of him. He felt anxious. His animal pressed against his psyche, comforting him with his presence.

The significance of the moment was not lost on him. The Wardens had waited a millennium to be called to act. *He* had been waiting his entire life.

"Do not fear the future, Troy," the Herald who had visited his Station said to him when he'd brought word that they had been activated, *"Your destiny awaits."*

Troy wondered if the old man referred to the Wardens finally being called to act, or if the elder spoke of yet another legend. Troy had been shocked to say the least when the Herald had entered their tidy little Station in Virginia Beach with his flowing white hair. After he told them the news, he turned to Troy and recited another old tale.

"Young Thunderbird, you are the first to return us to Terra. Do not doubt your worth. Your destiny has been written in the stars since before you were born, Troy Waman. Remember, a Warden discovers his true measure when his fated mate is thrust upon him."

Whatever the fuck that meant. Troy looked down at his phone, then to the street sign on the corner, and finally, to the faded numbers painted on the mailbox in front of the ramble of a house his map app had brought him to.

Fuck, am I thinking? Fated mates are myths. Stories made up so orphaned Shifters would sleep through the night. He scoffed at the thought. Memories of tales the head nurse, Sr. Maria, had told him at the training camp he'd called home for years invaded his brain.

Memories were pesky things. Sometimes eternal, and always fucking portable. But he was no longer a child. *No more stories, Sister. Now, I act.*

"A thousand years we've waited, and I'm walking into a fucking scene from a bad episode of *Hoarders*," Troy shook his head and frowned at the decrepit house that sat a few hundred feet away from him.

It was cold as fuck outside and his leather jacket did little to warm him. Avian Shifters did not carry around the same bulk as other types of Shifters. He ran hotter than normals, but the single digit temperature froze him to the bone.

True, he wasn't beefy like some of his fellow Shifters, but he was just as incredibly strong, and he was wicked fast. Much stronger than any average male. He paused briefly gauging the atmosphere. There was something off about the place. He scented *Magic* and something else. His Bird bristled beneath his skin. *Easy now.*

Lightning flashed in the darkened skies, allowing him to see the worn shingles, and cracked siding of the beaten-up colonial in greater detail. More than one window had been smashed and boarded up with cheap plywood.

If anything, it enhanced the creepy haunted house feel of the place. The porch sagged dangerously. He wondered how the place had managed to not be condemned by the town. One thing was certain, it was an ugly little turd of a house.

Who the hell put gray siding on their house anyway? Maybe it wasn't always that color. Maybe the owner liked gray. *Whatever.* He couldn't give two shits about the siding.

His only concern was the increased supernatural activity in the area over the past two weeks. Ever since the owner, a *Mrs. Renalda Curosi*, passed away. *A haunting?*

A creaking sound floated up to his ears and he stilled his movements. The sound developed into more of a *moaning* noise. An unearthly wail. It grew louder as the lightning continued to flash in the sky.

Troy had never seen a ghost. True, there were a lot of things in the universe he had never seen nor heard of, but that didn't make them any less real.

If ghosts were real, and they made noises, he imagined that pitiful wail was damn close to what it would sound like.

No such thing as ghosts. Yeah, well, most people had never heard of Shifters either. And yet, there he stood.

His Thunderbird shifted once more beneath his skin, the beast flexing his senses as the lightning in the air drew him to the surface. *No.* He told his other half. His human needed to be in control now. He walked across the street, keeping to the shadows.

Something was indeed off about the creepy old house. He inched further to the black door. The knocker was in the shape of a face or mask. No discernible features, just a vague impression of eyes, nose, and mouth. *Shadowland indeed.*

He listened with his enhanced hearing and frowned. There was a distinct voice somewhere beneath the moaning and creaking. A *female* voice. His curiosity was piqued.

From what he'd seen in her file, Mrs. Curosi was ninety-seven when she passed. Her closest living relative was a half-sister, a *Magdelena Kristos,* and she lived over three hours away in New Jersey. The half-sister was cut from Mrs. Curosi's will recently. She'd bequeathed her entire estate, house, bank account, and all her earthly belongings, to someone named *A. Kristos. Another sister? Maybe.*

Troy hadn't given it much thought until now. A crash sounded from inside the house. He perked up as the feminine voice he'd thought he'd heard earlier screamed in pain. *Time to act.*

Excerpt from Fangs For Nothin'
by C.D. Gorri

"Are you out of your mind?"

Xavier DuMont, Vampire and Prince of the Tenebris Clan out of DuMont, New Jersey, ran a hand over his face. It was almost five in the morning on Wednesday, and he was still going over the weekly requests and complaints.

He could not believe it. One after the other, he'd received dozens of requests for formal introductions for most of the eligible young females in the Clan by their parents or some family matchmaker or other. It was the 21st Century, and yet, the Vampires of the Tenebris Clan still thought he needed an arranged marriage to run things!

"No, Lucius, I assure you my mind is sound."

"How can you be thinking of going away? To some retreat? At this time of year! You know, the whole Clan is up in arms over the tax laws your father had set into motion before his demise. Some are questioning your right to rule. Then, there is still the matter of your mating—"

"Lucius, for the love of fuck! I know what is going on in my own Clan. I am even now revoking those tax laws, people will just have to be patient."

"And what about meeting with these young females? Maybe that will quell some of the unrest—"

"No! I am not inclined to take a mate at this time. My father's grave has barely begun to grow grass. There is no rush!"

"There is pressure though, sire," Lucius Redwing insisted.

He was Xavier's oldest and most reliable friend. At nearly three hundred years old, they'd known each other for a considerable length of time. Lucius had been his childhood companion when they'd fled France for the New World. After settling the town of DuMont, his father had not only been the most productive of the local normals, but he had taken over their branch of the Clan.

Breaking ties with the old regime, and establishing their own rule, the DuMonts had done exceedingly well. Of course, coming into the new century had been difficult for some, but Xavier was determined to do it, to breathe new life into the old-fashioned world of Vampires. He would see them succeed and blossom in this age that was simply exploding with technology.

"I know you have plans, sire. But the anxious mamas are already parading their daughters resumes as if they were applying for a job." Lucius grinned. He waved a manila envelope bursting with applications for audiences with him from the most prestigious Vampire families in all of DuMont.

"For fuck's sake, Luc. Get rid of them," Xavier growled, and ran a hand over his face.

"Now, now. Surely, you know enough not to disrespect tradition and courtesy. These families are your staunchest supporters. Without their aid, your ascension to leadership could be challenged. The right mate would stop all of that—"

"I will not be forced into this, Luc. If anyone wants to challenge me for the right to lead, then he or she can face me out in the open. Not hide behind some political game."

"But sire—"

"No. I will not be manipulated. You should know that of me, old friend."

"Yes. Of course." Lucius nodded, placing the hefty envelope on the corner of Xavier's desk.

Vampires did not always inherit the right to lead. Princes were not born but made. Wasn't that what his father had always said? And yet, royal blood flowed in his veins. And it was because of that blood —*his royal DuMont blood*—that so many hungry mamas yearned to tie one of their young to him for eternity.

Fortunately, Xavier had avoided them. He refused to be pressured to take any of the hungry misses for his mate, as of yet. But with his recent ascension, that pressure was now on full keel.

Shit and fuck.

"I've got an idea," Lucius said, thrusting a copy of *The Nightly News* at him.

"What is it, Luc? I am in no mood."

"Read there," his friend said, pointing at an article on the bottom left.

"A retreat? I haven't been on one of those since I was ninety."

"Yes, but remember the fun? I brought my *sheep* at the time, and you pouted because I wouldn't share her!"

"As I recall, she came quite willingly to my bed when summoned, Luc. Why do they still call them sheep? My gods, that is positively medieval!" he replied.

"In case normals see the newspaper, of course."

"Impossible. The Covens bespelled the paper to only go to supes."

"It has happened, Xavier. You know this as well as I."

"True. And Luc, I am sorry about Temple. That was your donor at the time, was it not?"

"Temple? Yes. Not to worry, sire. You always did woo the ladies without trying. Besides, now they have their own donors on hand. You do not need to bring one."

"You don't have to do that, you know."

"What?"

"Calling me sire."

"I do have to call you sire, *sire*. You are my Prince."

"Oh, do shut up. I am your friend, Luc. You've known me my entire life."

"Yes, sire."

"Luc," he growled his friend's name.

"Shall I make the arrangements then?"

"Fine. I will go to this retreat for the weekend if

only to shut you up. And to get away from all this."
He indicated the pile of correspondence.

"Very good, sire."

Excerpt from Code Wolf

"Are you fuckin' with me?"

"No, Randall, I assure you I am not fuckin' with you," Rafe Maccon eased his immense frame back into his oversized, black leather chair and narrowed his ice blue eyes at his Third and one of his oldest friends. How long had he known the man sitting in front of him?

Randall had come to Maccon City when Rafe was about ten, he looked the same then as he did now. Tall at six foot three inches, muscular, and more than a little intimidating to the Wolves under him with his long beard and equally long dark brown hair.

Rafe, however, was the Alpha. He was more amused than intimidated by his surly friend.

"A vacation?! What the fuck am I gonna do on a vacation? Come on, Rafe, this is bullshit!"

The door to Rafe's private office flew open and in strolled a very happy, very pregnant Charley Maccon, Rafe's wife. The Alpha's eyes glowed as they landed on his positively glowing mate. She wore a long, flowy dress. The shade was a pale-yellow color that, Randall admitted to himself, looked damn good with her creamy complexion and curly dark hair.

Their Alpha Female was quite something. There wasn't a Wolf Guard in the place who wouldn't lay down his/her life for her.

"Well, maybe you should consider a vacation to be a relaxing experience, Randy," she dropped a kiss on Randall's cheek and walked past him, over to her husband whom she kissed full on the mouth.

The way his Alpha's eyes homed in on her when she opened the door was nothing compared to the hungry gaze that followed her across the room.

Randall had noticed it took a while for Rafe to get used to his mate's habit of greeting everyone with a kiss or hug. Wolves were protective of their mates, but Randall thought his Alpha was doing an exceedingly good job of hiding his tension. Werewolves did not share very well.

Charley; however, had stood firm. That was the way she was raised, and she wasn't going to change for any, how had she put it? Neanderthal brow-beating husband, regardless of how cute his ass was!

Randall had no direct knowledge if the "cute ass" statement was true or not. And he didn't want to know. He liked Charley though, had from the beginning. He was musically inclined and often took to one of the common rooms to strum his guitar or play a few keys on the piano.

About the Author

C.D. Gorri is a USA Today Bestselling author of steamy paranormal romance and urban fantasy. She is the creator of the Grazi Kelly Universe.

Join her mailing list here: https://www.cdgorri.com/newsletter

An avid reader with a profound love for books and literature, when she is not writing or taking care of her family, she can usually be found with a book or tablet in hand. C.D. lives in her home state of New Jersey where many of her characters or stories are based. Her tales are fast paced yet detailed with satisfying conclusions.

If you enjoy powerful heroines and loyal heroes who face relatable problems in supernatural settings, journey into the Grazi Kelly Universe today. You will find sassy, curvy heroines and sexy, love-driven heroes who find their HEAs between the pages. Werewolves, Bears, Dragons, Tigers, Witches, Romani, Lynxes, Foxes, Thunderbirds, Vampires, and many more Shifters and supernatural creatures dwell within her worlds. The most important thing is every mate in this universe is fated, loyal, and true lovers always get their happily ever afters.

Want to know how it all began? Enter the Grazi Kelly Universe with Wolf Moon: A Grazi Kelly Novel or pick up Charley's Christmas Wolf and dive into the Macconwood Pack Novel Series today.

For a complete list of C.D. Gorri's books visit her website here:

https://www.cdgorri.com/complete-book-list/

Thank you and happy reading!

del mare alla stella,
    C.D. Gorri

Follow C.D. Gorri here:
    http://www.cdgorri.com
    https://www.facebook.com/Cdgorribooks

https://www.bookbub.com/authors/c-d-gorri
https://twitter.com/cgor22
https://instagram.com/cdgorri/
https://www.goodreads.com/cdgorri
https://www.tiktok.com/@cdgorriauthor